Big trouble . . .

Elizabeth had been frozen in her tracks, watching the terrible scene unfold. But now she knew it was time to take cover. This was war. She quickly ducked under the table as Sophia lunged for a bucket of orange paint, and Sarah dove for a bucket of black.

"You thug!" Sarah yelled as she reached into the bucket of black paint and tossed a handful of it in Sophia's direction.

"Stop it!" Elizabeth screamed from beneath the table.

But Sophia and Sarah were chasing each other around the table, each of them armed with fresh buckets.

"WHAT IS THE MEANING OF THIS?" a voice thundered from the doorway. Elizabeth looked up and saw Mr. Sweeney running into the room just as Sarah and Sophia let their paint buckets fly.

Elizabeth closed her eyes. She couldn't bear to watch. There were two loud "Splaaaaats," an outraged _____ then a terrible silence.

D1340232

SWEET VALLEY TWINS titles, published by Bantam Books.
Ask your bookseller for titles you have missed:

SWEET VALLEY TWINS SUPER CHILLERS

SWEET VALLEY TWINS SUPER EDITIONS

SWEET VALLEY TWINS

Sarah's Dad and Sophia's Mum

Written by
Jamie Suzanne

Created by
FRANCINE PASCAL

BANTAM BOOKS
TORONTO · NEW YORK · LONDON · SYDNEY · AUCKLAND

SARAH'S DAD AND SOPHIA'S MUM
A BANTAM BOOK 0 553 40402 6

Originally published in U.S.A. by Bantam Skylark Books

First publication in Great Britain

PRINTING HISTORY
Bantam edition published 1993

Conceived by Francine Pascal.

Produced by Daniel Weiss Associates, Inc., 33 West 17th Street, New York, NY 10011

Bantam Books are published by Transworld Publishers Ltd., 61–63 Uxbridge Road, Ealing, London W5 5SA, in Australia by Transworld Publishers (Australia) Pty. Ltd., 15–25 Helles Avenue, Moorebank, NSW 2170, and in New Zealand by Transworld Publishers (N.Z.) Ltd., 3 William Pickering Drive, Albany, Auckland.

Printed and bound in Great Britain by
Cox & Wyman Ltd., Reading, Berks.

Sarah's Dad
and
Sophia's Mum

One

◇

Jessica Wakefield chewed nervously on her fingernail as she watched Mr. Sweeney, the art teacher, walk to the front of the classroom. Art class was held once a week at Sweet Valley Middle School, and at the end of every class, each student tacked his or her picture to the front wall for Mr. Sweeney to critique.

"Hmmmm . . . interesting use of shapes," he said, examining a purple and black abstract painting. Then he moved on to the next picture, a collage made from cut-up magazine photos. "Very nice. Very nice indeed," he said with a smile. "Excellent treatment of theme and variation."

"That's mine," Ken Matthews said proudly.

"Shhhh," Jessica hissed. Mr. Sweeney had moved on and was looking at her picture. She hoped he would say something nice. Art was never her best subject, and today she had spent most of the class gossiping with her friends instead of concentrating on the assignment. In the last ten minutes she had worked furiously, slapping paint onto the paper as fast as possible. The result wasn't great, but Jessica thought it looked at least as good as most of the stuff she had seen in the Sweet Valley Museum of Modern Art.

Mr. Sweeney stared at Jessica's picture for a long time. Then he peered at the signature, shook his head, and sighed. "This is a wonderful example of something I've been trying to teach all of you . . ."

Jessica smiled proudly and sat up straighter. She loved compliments.

". . . which is that great art does not happen in a hurry," the teacher finished.

Several members of the class laughed, and Jessica felt her face turn red.

Oh, yeah? Jessica thought angrily. *What about "The Minute Waltz"?* But before she could say it out loud, Mr. Sweeney had moved on to the next picture, a painting of a mare and a foal.

"Lovely!" he exclaimed. "Very sensitive. Very thoughtful." He looked at the name in the corner. "Nice job, Elizabeth."

Jessica glared at Elizabeth. Elizabeth was Jessica's identical twin sister. Both girls were in the sixth grade at Sweet Valley Middle School. They both had long blond hair, blue-green eyes, and dimples in their left cheeks. But beyond that, Elizabeth and Jessica were as different as night and day.

Elizabeth was a serious student and she hoped to be a writer when she grew up. She was the editor of *The Sweet Valley Sixers*, the sixth-grade newspaper. When she wasn't working on the paper or having a long talk with one of her friends, she loved to curl up with a good mystery novel.

Jessica, on the other hand, liked gossiping about clothes, parties, and boys with her friends in the Unicorn Club. The Unicorns were a group of the prettiest and most popular girls at Sweet Valley Middle School. Their official club color was purple—the color of royalty. Each member was supposed to wear at least one purple article of clothing every day.

Elizabeth thought most of the girls in the Unicorn Club were snobs, and Jessica thought most of Elizabeth's friends were boring and much too serious. But despite their differences, Jessica and Elizabeth were the best of friends.

"I don't think Elizabeth's picture is so great," Jessica heard Dennis Cookman whisper to Ken. "Mr. Sweeney's just making a big deal about it because she's his pet."

Jessica had been a little annoyed about Elizabeth's getting so much praise, too. But when she overheard Dennis's remark, her blood began to boil. How dare he make fun of Elizabeth! "Shut up, Dennis," she hissed.

"Oh, sorry," he whispered sarcastically. "Are you and Elizabeth the only no-talents in the family? Or is everybody all thumbs?"

Jessica glared at Dennis. "For your information," she whispered, "every member of the Wakefield family is extremely talented."

Dennis snickered. "Oh, yeah? Name one Wakefield I might have heard of," he challenged.

Jessica opened her mouth to respond. Unfortunately, she couldn't think of any famous relatives. *Why couldn't my mom be a famous rock star like Brooke Dennis's, or even a TV newscaster like Amy Sutton's?* she thought desperately as she racked her brain for an answer.

She shrugged, and Dennis smiled triumphantly. Jessica knew that Ken Matthews wasn't a mean person, but even he started laughing.

I'll show them, Jessica thought with a sudden flash of inspiration. She gave them a smug smile. "Ever hear of Quake-Field Wakefield?"

"The star hitter for the Los Angeles Dodgers?" Ken exclaimed excitedly. Ken Matthews was a real baseball fan. He knew the name and vital statistics of every player on every team in the major leagues.

"He's my cousin," Jessica said. "A *distant* cousin, but definitely related." It wasn't true, but Ken and Dennis looked so impressed that Jessica was glad she had stretched the facts a little. After all, she figured that since his name *was* Wakefield, it *might* be true.

"Class!" Mr. Sweeney announced. "Now that we've completed this assignment, I want to remind you about the exciting new project we have to tackle. As you know, our library is in desperate need of sprucing up. Ms. Luster, our devoted librarian, has asked us to come up with something to cover the walls."

"Ten or twelve buckets of white paint should do it," Dennis said loudly.

The class laughed.

"That's the problem," Mr. Sweeney said. "There's no budget to paint the library until this summer. So in the meantime, I'd like this class to do a series of murals. Any suggestions for a theme?"

"Fashions of the future," Lila Fowler volunteered. Lila was one of Jessica's best friends and a fellow Unicorn.

"Baseball," Ken called out. He turned and smiled at Jessica.

"Food!"

"Pets!"

"Outer space!"

Mr. Sweeney noticed Elizabeth's raised hand. "Elizabeth?"

"What about ecology?" she suggested. "The theme could be people working together to save the planet. Something like . . . 'recycle now!' "

"That's a great idea," Mr. Sweeney said. "What do the rest of you think?"

Several members of the class began to applaud.

"Sounds like a popular idea," Mr. Sweeney said, smiling at Elizabeth. "OK then, listen up, everyone. I'm going to assign you to work together in groups of three. By the time we meet next week, I want each group to come up with its own approach to the 'recycle now' theme, and be ready to discuss it with me. I'm going to call out the groups right now so you'll have a few minutes to confer before the end of class."

Mr. Sweeney walked to his desk and picked up his stack of registration cards. He began to flip through them and call out names. "Jessica Wakefield, Ken Matthews, and Lloyd Benson. You three are group one."

Ugggh, Jessica thought, as Mr. Sweeney went on to the next group. She had hoped she would get to work with Lila or one of her other friends. If she had to be with guys, they could at least have been cute ones. She couldn't believe she'd been stuck with two geeks like Ken and Lloyd. Lloyd Benson was Sweet Valley Middle School's official computer nerd. And Jessica had had enough of nerds for a while. She had recently been in a special science program called SOAR! with Ken and Lloyd and a lot of the other nerdy types at school. She actually had ended up enjoying the class, but the Unicorns had given her a hard time about being in SOAR!

Ken headed over to the other side of the room where Lloyd was sitting. The two boys put their heads together for a few moments and then waved at Jessica. Jessica reluctantly joined them. "I told Lloyd about your cousin," Ken said eagerly.

"My cousin?" Jessica responded blankly.

"Quake-Field Wakefield," Ken said.

"Oh, *that* cousin," said Jessica. She had already forgotten about her little lie.

Ken's eyes were sparkling with excitement. "Wouldn't it be great if we could get him involved somehow? That way we could combine baseball and recycling."

"Maybe we could get him to pose while we paint a picture of him throwing a soda can into a recycling bin," Lloyd suggested.

"That's a great idea!" Ken exclaimed. "People drink tons of soda at baseball games. Just think of all the cans that could be recycled. We could paint him wearing his uniform, with the stadium behind him. Do you think you could talk him into posing for us, Jessica?"

Jessica bit her lip. Maybe her little white lie wasn't such a great idea after all. All she had wanted to do was shut Dennis Cookman up. "I don't know," she said. "He's pretty busy with the team and all. Why don't you just copy his picture from a photograph?"

Ken shook his head. "It wouldn't be the same. Besides, I bet he'd love to do it as a favor to his cousin."

As Jessica was trying to come up with a response, she felt a tap on her shoulder. She turned around to see Elizabeth standing behind her.

"Can I talk to you for a minute?" Elizabeth asked.

"Of course!" Jessica said with exaggerated enthusiasm. "Let's talk right now." She followed Elizabeth to the other side of the room.

"Are the Unicorns meeting at our house today?" Elizabeth asked.

"No. Why?"

"I thought I'd invite my group over this afternoon to start planning our mural," answered Elizabeth. "I'm working with Sarah Thomas and Sophia Rizzo."

"Double yuck!" Jessica said. She shook her head. "Geez, Elizabeth, we both had bad luck on this one. I'm stuck with Ken and Lloyd. That's almost as bad as having to work with Sarah and Sophia."

"What's wrong with Sarah and Sophia?" Elizabeth demanded.

Jessica rolled her eyes. "Sarah Thomas is a big baby, and Sophia is a troublemaker."

"That's not true," Elizabeth said. "Why do you have to be so mean about people?"

"I'm not mean. I'm honest," Jessica replied, folding her arms and preparing for an argument. But before Elizabeth could say anything else, Lila came rushing over.

"Hey, Jess, guess who I got stuck with? Melissa McCormick and Dennis Cookman."

"I know how you feel," Jessica said sympathetically. She caught Elizabeth glaring at her. "Um . . . I mean, Melissa's really nice," she added quickly.

"At least Melissa is willing to stick with my fashions-of-the-future idea. We're going to do futuristic fashion drawings of clothes made out of recycled materials. Not that Melissa knows much about fashion. Did you get a look at that skirt she's wearing? I'll bet it's two years old at least." Lila giggled. "I guess she's already into recycled clothes."

Jessica saw Elizabeth shaking her head. Even Jessica had to admit that Lila could be pretty snobby at times. She lived alone with her father, who was one of the wealthiest people in Sweet Valley. Mr. Fowler had to travel a lot on business, and he tried to make up for leaving Lila alone so often by buying her everything she wanted—no matter what it cost.

"Melissa McCormick may not be a fashion plate," Lila continued, "but at least she knows more about clothes than Dennis Cookman. He hates my idea. He'd rather work with boys. So if it's okay with everybody in your group, he'll switch places with you."

"Great," Jessica said. "I'd much rather work with you and Melissa. Let me just tell Ken and Lloyd." But when she turned, she saw that the two boys were standing right behind her.

"We heard," Ken said with a grin. "And the answer is no way. We're not giving up on our baseball idea. Since you're Quake-Field Wakefield's cousin, you're the only one who can help us get it done." He threw his arm over Jessica's shoulder. "Like it or not, we're a team."

Jessica rolled her eyes, wishing she had just kept her big mouth shut.

"Quake-Field Wakefield is your cousin?" Lila exclaimed.

Jessica shot a nervous look in her sister's direction. Elizabeth looked as surprised as Lila did.

"Yes, but it's not something we talk about much at home," Jessica said.

"It's not something we talk about at all," Elizabeth put in with a mischievous smile.

Jessica frowned at her twin, silently willing her to play along.

"If Quake-Field Wakefield were a member of my family, I'd make sure everybody knew about it," Lloyd said.

"Well, he's not," Jessica snapped. "And if you'll excuse us, my sister and I were discussing some personal family business."

She grabbed Elizabeth's sleeve and pulled her over to a quiet corner. "Stop laughing!" she commanded.

"I thought you said you were honest," Elizabeth said.

In spite of herself, Jessica had to smile. "So I stretched the truth a little."

"*Stretched* it? Try bent, folded, and mutilated it. What made you tell such a big lie?"

Jessica frowned. "Our family honor depended on it."

Elizabeth laughed so hard she almost choked.

"It's true," Jessica insisted. "Dennis Cookman was saying the Wakefields were a big bunch of no-talents. I was just trying to shut him up."

"How are you going to shut him up now? The story's going to be all over school by tomorrow."

Jessica shrugged. "I don't know. I'll think of something. Just promise me that you won't give me away."

"I won't lie for you," Elizabeth said seriously. "But I won't volunteer any information, either. If anybody asks me, I'll just say I don't know very much about it."

Jessica smiled. "Thanks, Lizzie. Besides," she added brightly, "the story might be true!"

"You're right," Elizabeth agreed. "And there *might* be life on Mars. The Loch Ness Monster *might* be living in Sweet Valley Lake. Come to think of it, the earth *might* be flat after all. In fact, we *might* be . . ."

"Oh, shut up," Jessica said grumpily.

Two

◇

That afternoon after school, Elizabeth hurried around the living room picking up newspapers and straightening the sofa cushions. She wanted the room to look nice when Sophia and Sarah arrived.

In spite of what Jessica said, Elizabeth liked both girls. Although Sophia and Sarah hardly knew each other, she hoped they would like each other. Elizabeth felt sure that the three of them would make a good team.

Unfortunately, Jessica wasn't the only one at Sweet Valley Middle School who thought Sophia Rizzo was a troublemaker. Lots of kids steered clear of Sophia because of her older brother's bad reputation. Tony Rizzo had been in trouble with the police more than once and had gone to a reform school for a while. Mr. Rizzo had run out on the family two years earlier, and Elizabeth knew that Mrs. Rizzo had had a hard time keeping the family going.

But she also knew that Tony was back at home and attending Sweet Valley High regularly, and Mrs. Rizzo had found a job she liked. The family really seemed to be turning around.

Still, the struggles of the past had left their mark on Sophia. She could seem kind of tough sometimes, but Elizabeth knew it was just a defensive pose. Underneath the prickly exterior, Sophia was one of the smartest and nicest girls at Sweet Valley Middle School.

Sarah Thomas wasn't a great student, but Elizabeth had to admit that if her mother had died suddenly, like Mrs. Thomas had two years earlier, she would have a hard time concentrating on school, too. Ever since her mother's death, Sarah had become more and more timid and shy, preferring to spend weekends with her father rather than hanging out with kids from school.

But Elizabeth knew that Sarah could be outgoing and outspoken when she wanted to be. And she also knew that Sarah had a lot of artistic talent.

Elizabeth jumped when she heard the doorbell. She gave the pillows a last thump and ran to the door. When she opened it she was surprised to see both girls standing on the doorstep.

"Hi," she said, smiling. "Did you two come together?"

Sarah threw Sophia a nervous look. "No. We just happened to arrive at the same time. My dad was going to drive me over, but it was such a nice day that I decided to walk."

"I walked, too," Sophia said. "Not that I had any choice. My mom has to work and can't just drop everything to chauffeur me around."

"My father works, too," Sarah said defensively.

Elizabeth stared at the two girls. Sarah, in her pink mohair sweater and feathery curls, couldn't have looked more different from Sophia in her no-nonsense black jeans and turtleneck. And they looked as if they were squaring off for a fight.

"Why don't you both come inside?" Elizabeth said quickly, hoping to smooth things over.

Sarah and Sophia followed Elizabeth into the living room and sat down at opposite ends of the sofa. Elizabeth gave them a big smile.

"Maybe we should talk a little bit about what we want our mural to look like," she began. "It would be nice if we could each include our interests."

"OK by me," Sophia said briskly.

"Fine," agreed Sarah.

Silence.

Elizabeth gave them what she hoped was an encouraging smile. Sarah folded her arms over her chest, and Sophia stared sullenly at the ceiling, tapping a pencil on her knee.

Suddenly, the living room seemed awfully hot to Elizabeth. She pulled on the neck of her T-shirt, racking her brain for a way to get the conversation started.

Since neither one of the girls seemed willing to volunteer any information, Elizabeth plunged on ahead. "Sarah, did you know that Sophia is a really good writer?"

"Oh," Sarah said in a polite but disinterested voice.

"She contributes a lot of articles to *The Sixers*," Elizabeth added, hoping Sophia would pick up the conversational ball.

But Sophia continued to stare at the ceiling, tapping away at her knee with the pencil.

"Are you interested in writing, Sarah?" Elizabeth asked.

"Not really," Sarah said. "I'm more interested in design and fashion."

For the first time, Sophia turned her attention to Sarah. She gave her a long look that seemed to take in the carefully curled hair, the pink lipstick, and the matching nail polish.

"Maybe Sarah should think about joining the Unicorns," she said with the faintest of sneers.

Sarah glared at Sophia.

"For your information," Sarah said icily, "I am not into unicorns. I collect rainbows."

Elizabeth sat up and leaned forward. Maybe they were about to make a breakthrough. "Rainbows," she said excitedly. "How do you collect rainbows?"

Sarah smiled a little. "I have all kinds of posters and pens and notebooks and sweatshirts with rainbows on them. And whenever my father goes out of town, he brings me something for my collection. I have a rainbow mug from Europe, some rainbow jewelry from New York, and lots of other things."

Sarah's face was pink with pleasure, and her voice was full of genuine enthusiasm.

"Maybe we could incorporate a rainbow in our mural design," Elizabeth said.

"Too babyish," Sophia said decisively.

"Babyish!" cried Sarah.

"Well, we don't have to decide right now," Elizabeth said quickly. "Why don't we have something to eat first? I thought we could make some slice-and-bake cookies."

"Great," Sarah said. "Do you have chocolate chip?"

Sophia grimaced. "Yuck. Too sweet. Don't you have oatmeal or something?"

"Why don't we just chew on some cardboard?" Sarah suggested in a sarcastically sweet voice. "It's not too sweet, and it's probably better for you."

"What do you have against healthy food?" Sophia demanded.

"Nothing," snapped Sarah. "Eat what you want. I'm not hungry anyway."

"Me neither," Sophia countered.

Elizabeth sighed. *This is a nightmare*, she decided. What was making these two perfectly nice, intelligent people behave like little kids? "Why don't we just get to work," she said.

"OK," Sophia said eagerly. She opened her notebook and stuck a pencil through her tangled ponytail. "I've made some notes on the project. Now we all know that unless we recycle things like cans and bottles and boxes, we're going to do serious damage to the planet. So how about if we draw a big geometric pyramid made of old wrecked cars and bottles and cans and stuff. Underneath the pyramid, we'll show a squashed globe."

Elizabeth smiled. When Sophia got interested in a subject and dropped her tough-girl act, she was really pretty easy to like. She looked over at Sarah. Sarah was frowning.

"Too depressing," Sarah said.

"Well, life isn't all rainbows," Sophia said hotly.

"I never said it was," Sarah argued. "I just

think we should take a more decorative approach. The point of this project is to cheer up the library."

"The point is to make a statement about the importance of recycling," Sophia corrected.

"Does something have to be ugly to make a statement?" Sarah asked, looking pointedly at Sophia's stained and faded turtleneck.

Sophia flushed and quickly shoved her ink-smeared hands into her pockets. Sophia was very talented, but clothes and makeup were definitely not her thing.

Sarah flushed, too, and bit her lip. Elizabeth could tell that she wished she hadn't made such a cutting remark. But it was too late to take it back.

"Why don't we call it quits for today," Elizabeth suggested quietly. "We'll all give the project some more thought and then get together again later this week."

"How about Thursday?" Sophia asked.

"That's fine," Elizabeth said. "But my mom works at home on Thursday afternoons. She's a part-time interior designer, and when she works at home, she likes to spread out her sketchbooks and stuff in the living room. So I don't think we can work here."

"We can work at my house," Sophia offered.

Sarah shot Elizabeth a worried look.

Elizabeth had a feeling she knew what Sarah was thinking—that the Rizzos were a troubled family from the wrong side of town. But Elizabeth had been to the Rizzos' many times and knew that they were a really nice family and lived in a perfectly nice house. Once Sarah got to know them, she'd like them, too.

Elizabeth smiled. "That sounds great. Sarah and I can walk over together."

"OK then," Sophia said gruffly.

Elizabeth walked the two girls to the front door and watched as they walked off in two different directions. She shut the door, trudged into the living room, and threw herself facedown on the sofa. She couldn't help wondering if Sarah and Sophia could possibly finish the mural without killing each other first.

"What's the matter with you?" asked Jessica, bounding into the living room a few minutes later.

"Don't even ask," Elizabeth answered. She didn't feel like listening to Jessica say "I told you so."

But Jessica wasn't waiting for an answer. She was busily climbing up on a wing chair and reaching for a book on the top shelf on the bookcase. "Got it," she said, as she pulled down a thick volume. She sat down in the chair and started turning the pages.

Elizabeth rolled over and gave her sister a curious look. Books weren't usually of much interest to Jessica.

Just then the front door opened, and Mr. and Mrs. Wakefield came into the living room carrying bags of groceries. They were followed by the twins' older brother, Steven, who was a freshman at Sweet Valley High.

"Good grief!" Mr. Wakefield exclaimed. "Have we stepped into some kind of parallel universe? Unless my eyes deceive me, I think I see Jessica poring over a book and Elizabeth lying around on the couch."

"Very funny," Jessica said sourly.

Elizabeth giggled. "Strange but true."

"What are you reading, Jessica?" Mrs. Wakefield asked. "It looks like the Wakefield family genealogy that Aunt Harriet had bound for us last Christmas."

"That's exactly what it is," Jessica said. "I'm just trying to see if we have any famous relatives."

"You mean besides me?" Steven asked. Steven was the star of the Sweet Valley High junior varsity basketball team.

"I mean famous outside of Sweet Valley High," Jessica said with a frown. "Famous as in Quake-Field Wakefield. Is there any chance at all that we're related?" she asked her father.

"Not as far as I know," Mr. Wakefield said,

laughing. "But if you find a connection, let me know. Maybe we can get some free baseball tickets."

Steven reached over and picked up the sports section of the newspaper from the floor. "Wasn't that Tony Rizzo's sister I saw walking down the street?"

Elizabeth sat up and nodded. "Sophia and I and Sarah Thomas are doing an art project together. We had our first meeting today."

"How did it go?" Mrs. Wakefield asked.

"Not too well," Elizabeth admitted. "Sarah and Sophia didn't really get along. I have a feeling this isn't going to be much fun."

Behind Mrs. Wakefield's back, Elizabeth could see Jessica grinning and mouthing the words "I told you so."

"Oh, shut up," Elizabeth said, ignoring the surprised looks on her parents' and Steven's faces.

Three

◇

"We're almost there," Elizabeth said to Sarah.

It was Thursday afternoon, and the two of them were walking from Sarah's house to the Rizzos'. It wasn't a very long walk in terms of distance. But the two neighborhoods were miles apart in other ways.

In Sarah's neighborhood, the houses were large and handsome with neatly tended front yards. Expensive cars were parked in most of the driveways. In the Rizzos' neighborhood, the houses were much smaller. Many of them were badly in need of a fresh coat of paint and some new shingles. Most of the tiny front yards were scraggly and overgrown from lack of care.

"This doesn't look like a very nice neighborhood," Sarah said, sounding nervous. "Maybe it's not safe to walk around here. I could call my father and have him drive us the rest of the way."

"It really is a safe neighborhood," Elizabeth said. "Look, there's Sophia's house right across the street."

Sarah stared at the house for a long time. Even Elizabeth had to admit that the outside did not look reassuring. Paint was peeling off the side of the house, and there were some loose boards stacked on the front porch. But Sarah didn't even seem to notice the beautifully planted window boxes or the red and pink roses growing in the flower beds beside the front walk.

"I'm not sure I want to go in," Sarah said suddenly in a defiant voice. "I don't care if Sophia is your friend. I think she's awful, and this house looks positively gross. I'm not going inside, and you can't make me!"

Jessica's right, Elizabeth thought. Sarah Thomas *was* a big baby. And she was acting like a real snob, too. Elizabeth almost felt like telling her to get lost.

However, Elizabeth knew that getting angry with Sarah wouldn't accomplish anything. If Sarah was going to act like a baby, Elizabeth was just going to have to baby her. She took a deep breath.

"You don't have to go in if you don't want to," she said in a soothing voice. "But believe me, there's nothing to be afraid of. I know the house looks a little shabby from the outside. That's because the Rizzos don't have a lot of money and Mrs. Rizzo works full-time. Let's go inside, and if you still feel uncomfortable, you can call your father to come get you."

Sarah kicked her foot moodily against the curb and stared again at the house. Her lower lip trembled, and her eyes looked dangerously watery.

Elizabeth held her breath, hoping with all her might that Sarah wasn't going to start crying. *If Sarah starts to cry*, she thought in frustration, *I don't know what I'll do!*

Finally, Sarah straightened her shoulders and pulled in her lower lip. "OK," she said grudgingly. "But if I don't like it, I'm calling my father right away."

Elizabeth sighed with relief and quickly led the way to the Rizzos' front door. Before she could ring the bell, Sophia flung open the door. She gave Elizabeth a big smile.

"Hi. I saw you two talking outside and thought you might be changing your minds about coming inside." Sophia was smiling, but Elizabeth could hear the defensive tone in her voice. Sophia knew that her house wasn't as nice as the other girls'.

"I wasn't sure this was the right house," Elizabeth said, watching Sarah carefully. "I haven't been here in a while." No matter what Sarah decided to do, Elizabeth hoped she wouldn't hurt Sophia's feelings.

But Elizabeth quickly realized she didn't need to worry. Sarah was looking around the room with obvious pleasure.

"This is just . . . beautiful," she breathed. And it was. Mrs. Rizzo obviously had a good eye for color and design. None of the furnishings were expensive, but everything had been carefully chosen. There were bright and vibrant colors everywhere. Plaids and floral prints seemed somehow to blend perfectly. Polished tabletops held attractive and interesting items, and warm rugs were scattered across the floor. Being in the Rizzos' living room was like being inside a jewelry box. Everywhere Elizabeth looked, there was something pretty.

"My mom's good at things like decorating and putting clothes together," Sophia said. "Too bad it didn't rub off on me."

Elizabeth smiled. "You just have different interests, that's all. Like recycling, for instance. Speaking of which . . ." she began, hoping to get the conversation going in the right direction, "I had an idea."

The three of them sat down on the sofa, and Sophia and Sarah looked at Elizabeth attentively.

"Last year a birthday party I went to had a

caricature artist. You know, that's a person who draws cartoon portraits. Anyway, the artist asked each person what her special interest or hobby was. If the person said she loved horses, the artist drew a cartoon picture of her on a horse. And if she said she loved playing the piano, the artist drew a cartoon of her sitting at a piano."

Sophia and Sarah both looked interested, so Elizabeth took a deep breath and went on. "Anyway, I was thinking that our mural could be a series of caricatures of the people in our class. Each person's special interest or club could be represented and everyone will be helping to hold up a banner that says 'Recycle Now.' "

Sarah nodded and smiled. "I think it's a great idea. It's a way of saying that everybody, no matter what they plan to do with their life, should recycle and help keep the planet clean."

"I think we could have a lot of fun with it," Elizabeth said. "For instance, the music club could be shown playing funny instruments made out of recycled materials."

Sarah nodded. "The Boosters could be waving pom-poms made out of recycled newspapers. And the shop class could be making strange furniture out of old bicycle parts and things like that."

Elizabeth noticed that Sophia didn't look very enthusiastic. She was sitting back and frowning.

"I think it's a great idea," she said finally. "But there's one big problem. None of us can draw well enough to do the caricatures."

Elizabeth smiled. "Sarah can. She draws really well. But since we usually do abstract work in art class, she doesn't get much chance to show off her talent."

Sarah blushed, and Sophia looked at her skeptically.

"Do you really think you can do it?" Sophia asked.

Sarah reached over to the coffee table and grabbed Sophia's notebook and pencil. She began to draw rapidly with bold strokes. In less than a minute, she held up her drawing, and both Elizabeth and Sophia gasped. It was a wonderful caricature of Elizabeth wearing an old-fashioned pressman's hat.

"It looks just like her!" Sophia exclaimed.

"Oh, no!" Elizabeth protested, laughing. Like all caricature artists, Sarah had exaggerated Elizabeth's features in a cartoon fashion. Her blond ponytail stuck out from beneath the hat like a horse's tail. Her large blue-green eyes were the size of dinner plates, and her face had a very serious, but comic, expression on it.

Sarah giggled. Even Sophia was laughing now.

"It's great," Sophia said, clapping her hands. "If Sarah can do pictures like this of everybody, we'll have the best mural in the class."

"I can do it," Sarah said proudly. "We'll all work together to come up with the ideas. Then I can do the sketches in pencil, and all three of us can work on filling in the color."

"Let's get started," Sophia said, reaching for another notebook. "Ideas?"

"I think we should put Rick Hunter in the center," Sarah said. "He's into weight lifting. He could be holding up the banner."

"Gag!" Sophia screeched. "He's all muscle and no brains. If we're going to put anybody in the center, it should be Patrick Morris. He's smart and really nice, and I've heard him talk about ecology a lot. He cares about keeping the planet in good shape."

"He should quit worrying about the planet and worry about getting *himself* in good shape. His arms look like toothpicks." Sarah giggled. "I could do a really funny drawing of him."

Sophia glowered. "Just try it," she challenged, balling her hands into fists.

Sarah glared at Sophia, and Sophia glared back.

Oh, no, Elizabeth thought. *Here we go again.*

"Let's not argue," she pleaded. "We don't

have time. Let's put Rick on one end and Patrick on the other. They can each be holding up an end of the banner."

"Fine," Sophia said curtly.

"Whatever," Sarah muttered.

"OK then," Elizabeth said. "Let's come up with some more ideas."

Sophia located a list of class members, and she and Elizabeth began making notes next to each name. Soon, they were so absorbed in their work that they forgot all about Sarah, who sat in her chair quietly sketching.

"I think that's it," Sophia said when she and Elizabeth had gotten to the bottom of the list. "We've come up with a fun way of showing everybody in the class. Now we need Sarah to figure out how it all fits together."

Elizabeth looked over at Sarah, who was smiling down at the sketch she had been working on. "Let's see what you've got," Elizabeth said.

Sarah hugged the pad to her chest. "This is something private." She giggled. "I don't think I want to show it to you."

"Come on," Elizabeth coaxed. "I'm sure it's fantastic."

Sarah just giggled again.

"It's probably a picture of Rick Hunter," Sophia said with a laugh. "Come on, Elizabeth. Let's take a look."

Elizabeth and Sophia leaped on the giggling Sarah and wrestled the pad from her.

But when Elizabeth and Sophia looked at the drawing, their laughter came to a sudden stop. Sophia's face flushed red with anger.

Sarah's sketch was a caricature of Sophia, and it was far from flattering. Sarah had drawn Sophia wearing a leather jacket covered with zippers and brass knuckles on her fingers. Her blue jeans were dirty and little wiggly lines around her seemed to indicate that she smelled bad.

"Well, thanks a lot," Sophia said.

"I draw 'em as I see 'em," Sarah said stubbornly.

"Oh, yeah?" Sophia responded. "Well, here's how I see you." Sophia grabbed the pad, sketched quickly, and then turned the pad around for the girls to see.

Her drawing wasn't nearly as good as Sarah's, but the character she had sketched looked like a big, dumb baby doll with tears rolling down its cheeks. There was no doubt that it was meant to be Sarah.

Elizabeth felt her cheeks getting hot with anger. *What is it with these two?* she thought. *They bring out the absolute worst in each other.* After five minutes in each other's company, Sarah began to act like a two-year-old, and Sophia began to act like the tough bully in Sarah's drawing.

Elizabeth grabbed the pad and began her own sketch. "Here's how I see the two of you," she said angrily. She held up the pad to show them a picture of two squalling infants wearing diapers and kicking at each other with little high-top shoes.

In spite of themselves, Sophia and Sarah both began to laugh.

"I'm sorry," Sophia said.

"Me, too," Sarah admitted.

"Then can we just put our differences aside for right now and get on with the project?" Elizabeth pleaded.

Both girls nodded.

"Let's go over the ideas," Sarah said. "Then I can work on the sketch at home. I've got a long piece of mural paper there. If I can finish it by next Tuesday, we can start painting it in class."

Elizabeth sighed. Maybe they finally were making some progress. But it was uphill all the way.

"It's not funny," Elizabeth said, frowning. It was later that night. Jessica was sitting on her sister's bed laughing as Elizabeth told her about her afternoon with Sarah and Sophia.

"Yes, it is," Jessica argued with a grin. "I just wish you'd brought home the sketches they drew of each other."

"It's amazing," Elizabeth said. "They're both smart. They're both funny. But they're so awful when they're together. They seem to have absolutely nothing in common."

"Not true," Jessica countered. "They're both stubborn."

Elizabeth put her hands on her hips.

"I know," Jessica said, starting to laugh again. "I'm shutting up right now." She ducked into the bathroom that led to her room and quickly closed the door.

But Elizabeth could still hear her laughing on the other side of the bathroom door. In spite of herself, Elizabeth began to laugh, too.

Four

◇

I wish I had never opened my big mouth, Jessica thought as she hurried to art class on Tuesday. She had spent the whole day fielding questions about her famous "cousin," Quake-Field Wakefield.

She had studied every page of the family genealogy book, but she hadn't found a connection with Quake-Field Wakefield anywhere. But she was keeping that to herself. If everybody found out she had lied, she'd be completely and totally humiliated.

"Jessica!" she heard a voice call.

Jessica turned and saw Janet Howell walking toward her. Janet was an eighth-grader and the president of the Unicorns. She was probably the most important girl at Sweet Valley Middle School. Jessica knew she would be late for class if she stopped to talk, but she figured it was worth it to stay on Janet's good side.

"Hi, Janet," Jessica said. "What's up?"

"I heard the most interesting news," Janet said in her best club-president voice. "Someone told me that you're related to Quake-Field Wakefield. Why haven't you mentioned it to me? You know the Unicorns are very interested in anything that reflects well on its members."

That was true. No Unicorn ever hesitated to brag—to each other or to anybody else who would listen.

"Well," Jessica replied, thinking fast. "It's not something we like to talk about."

"Why not?" Janet demanded.

"Ummmm . . ." Jessica's brain was working fast and furious. "It's . . . well . . . it's like a family feud. Our branch of the Wakefields doesn't speak to his branch of the Wakefields."

Janet's eyes were wide with interest.

Jessica paused for a moment, pulling the pieces of her story together. "You see, his great-great-great-grandfather, who was my great-great-great-grandfather's brother, fell in love with the woman who was supposed to marry his brother, *my* great-great-great-grandfather. They married secretly and didn't invite anyone in the family to the wedding." Jessica smiled. She was really cooking now. "Then they ran away—on a ship I think—

and nobody saw them again for thirty years. My great-great-great-grandfather was so heartbroken that he locked himself up in a tower and eventually died of a broken heart. He never forgave them, and after his death, he was buried on a lonely prairie beside the body of his first wife, who was my great-great-great-grandmother. As far as my family is concerned, Quake-Field's great-great-great-grandfather and great-great-great-grandmother *murdered* my great-great-great-grandfather. Ever since then, we haven't spoken to anyone on that side of the family."

By the time Jessica finished her story, she was exhausted. And she wasn't completely sure that she had included the right number of "greats" in her big finish.

Janet looked a little cross-eyed, but sympathetic. "That's a wonderful story," she said with a sigh. "And I can certainly see why you wouldn't want to have anything to do with him. I was going to suggest that we put a notice in the school paper about your relationship. But now, I don't think he deserves any more publicity."

Jessica let out a sigh of relief and before she could say another word, the bell rang.

"I've got to go," Janet said impatiently. "And Jessica, the next time you have a story like that, I really wish you would save it for lunch instead of making me late for class."

* * *

Mr. Sweeney was busy talking to Elizabeth's group when Jessica raced into the art room. His back was turned, so Jessica was able to sneak in without being noticed.

"Here she is," Ken said as Jessica joined him and Lloyd at one of the long work tables. "Have you called Quake-Field yet? Is he going to pose for us?"

Jessica pursed her lips. "No, I haven't. And I'm not going to. I have my reasons for not wanting to contact him. And frankly," she added icily, "they're none of your business."

"Saving the planet is everybody's business," Ken argued. "I'm sure if you called him, he'd want to do his part to help."

"Believe me," Jessica said. "He wouldn't want to hear from me any more than I would want to hear from him. His branch of the family and my branch of the family haven't spoken for generations. His great-great-great . . ."—Jessica had to stop and think. Was it three or four "greats"? Three was plenty, she decided—". . . grandfather betrayed mine."

"That's terrible," Ken said, frowning.

"I knew you'd understand," Jessica said. "So now you know why I can't call him."

"No, that's not what I meant," Ken said. "I

meant it's terrible that your family has let some moldy old feud keep you apart. It's up to you to reconcile the two halves of the family, Jessica." Ken leaned forward, his face earnest. "Families should stick together," he said seriously. "Why don't you write Quake-Field a letter and lay this thing to rest?"

"I can't," Jessica insisted. "It would be like betraying the honor of my family."

Ken and Lloyd looked at each other and shook their heads.

"How can we hope for world peace when people can't even get along with their own families?" Lloyd asked.

"If you don't mind," Jessica said haughtily, "I'd rather not discuss this any further. It's very painful for my family." Jessica kept her expression carefully aloof. But inside, she was dying to giggle. *I sure pulled that off*, she congratulated herself.

Elizabeth, Sarah, and Sophia were busy conferring with Mr. Sweeney on their mural design. True to her promise, Sarah had finished sketching the outlines at home and brought the finished product into class. Mr. Sweeney was delighted. "Excellent!" he said for about the tenth time. "Truly excellent. It's funny. It's professional. And it makes a very eloquent statement. Congratulations to all of you."

The three girls smiled at each other.

"It looks to me as if you three are ready to start painting," Mr. Sweeney said. "I'm going to move you into the empty studio next door." He carefully rolled up the mural paper and motioned for the girls to follow him.

The room next door was smaller than the art room. But it had a long table to work on and plenty of room for the three girls to spread out and paint.

Mr. Sweeney found them several large pots of paint, lots of brushes, and some rags. "You three are way ahead of the others," he said, smiling. "Ms. Luster is going to be thrilled. I wouldn't be surprised if you were finished by the end of the week. Good luck." He hurried back out to the main classroom.

Sarah unrolled the paper on the table.

"You really did a super job," Elizabeth said. "You took every one of our ideas and brought them to life."

"Not *every* one," Sophia said. "You forgot to include Mr. Bowman. He's my favorite teacher."

Sarah rolled her eyes and reached for her pencil. "Oh, all right," she grumbled. "I'll put him in right now."

Sarah quickly sketched in a cartoon of Mr. Bowman in the background.

"You're making him look ridiculous," Sophia protested.

"I am not," Sarah said.

"You are, too," Sophia insisted. "Mr. Bowman is a lot taller than that. And he may not have the best taste in clothes, but you don't have to make him look like a clown."

Sarah's face clouded over, and Elizabeth could see that they were headed for another stupid argument.

"Sophia may have a point," she said hastily. "We wouldn't want to hurt his feelings. Since it's so easy for you to draw," she added diplomatically, "maybe you could just erase the ruffle around his neck and make him a little bit taller."

Sarah frowned, but she erased the big ruffle around Mr. Bowman's neck and altered the sketch so that he didn't look quite so short. "*Now* can we start painting?" she asked impatiently.

"Sure," Sophia said. She dipped a brush into a pot of blue paint and prepared to fill in the sky.

"Oh," Sarah said quickly, "make sure you leave room in that corner for the rainbow."

Sophia dropped her brush into the paint bucket with a "splat."

"What rainbow?" she demanded.

"The rainbow that's going in that corner," Sarah replied stubbornly.

"No rainbow!" Sophia declared.

"Says who?"

"Says me," Sophia said calmly. She picked up the paintbrush and began to brush thick blue paint all over the corner of the paper.

"Don't paint there!" Sarah squeaked. "I told you, that's where the rainbow is going."

"HAH!" Sophia barked, piling more paint in the corner.

Sarah leaned forward to snatch the brush from Sophia's hand. But just as she did, Sophia moved her hand away and Sarah's hand smacked into the bucket of blue paint.

The bucket flew backward, and the next thing Elizabeth knew, blue paint was splattered all over Sophia's face and hair and was dripping down the front of her blouse.

Sophia was too stunned to react for a moment. But she recovered quickly. Snatching up a bucket of white paint and a bucket of red, she snarled, "Think pink, princess," and heaved both buckets in Sarah's direction.

Sarah let out a shriek as the red and white paint splashed over her. "Oh!" she gasped. "How *dare* you!"

Elizabeth had been frozen in her tracks, watching the terrible scene unfold. But now she knew it was time to take cover. This was war. She quickly ducked under the table as Sophia lunged for a bucket of orange paint, and Sarah dove for a bucket of black.

"You thug!" Sarah yelled as she reached into the bucket of black paint and tossed a handful of it in Sophia's direction.

"Splatttt!" went the bucket of orange paint as Sophia threw it at Sarah.

"Splatttt!" went the bucket of black paint as Sarah threw it at Sophia.

"Stop it!" Elizabeth screamed from beneath the table.

But Sophia and Sarah were chasing each other around the table, each of them armed with fresh buckets.

"WHAT IS THE MEANING OF THIS?" a voice thundered from the doorway. Elizabeth looked up and saw Mr. Sweeney running into the room just as Sarah and Sophia let their paint buckets fly.

Elizabeth closed her eyes. She couldn't bear to watch. There were two loud "splaaaaaats," an outraged shout, and then a terrible silence.

The silence went on and on. There wasn't a sound in the room except for the slow and steady drip of paint.

Finally, Elizabeth couldn't stand it anymore. She opened her eyes and immediately wished she had kept them shut. Mr. Sweeney was covered with paint from head to toe. Red paint dripped from his shoulders. Green paint oozed down his head, into his collar, and out the sleeves of his coat. He looked like a melted Christmas candle.

Sarah and Sophia could only stand there in silence, their eyes round with horror.

Elizabeth held her breath. She had never heard of a teacher actually *killing* a student. But there was a first time for everything, and Mr. Sweeney looked angry enough to kill. Elizabeth was glad she was safely under the table.

Without saying a word, Mr. Sweeney removed a handkerchief from his back pocket, took off his glasses, and began slowly to wipe them clean. "Come with me," he said in an awful whisper. "All of you."

Elizabeth reluctantly crawled out from under the table. When she saw the mural sketch, she felt a lump rise in her throat. It was ruined. All of Sarah's wonderful drawing was absolutely ruined.

She turned to follow Mr. Sweeney to the principal's office.

"Now then," said Mr. Clark, the principal. "Who is responsible for this?" He glared at each of them, one by one. "Elizabeth," he said, "I must say I'm surprised at you."

Elizabeth bit her lip and lowered her eyes.

"It wasn't her fault," Sophia said. "She wasn't involved at all."

"That's right," Sarah agreed softly. "It was my fault, and Sophia's. We got into an argument and . . ." Sarah's voice trailed off weakly.

". . . and you ruined Mr. Sweeney's clothing. You vandalized the art studio. You've gotten yourselves into some very big trouble," Mr. Clark finished for her. He quickly scribbled out two notes, stuffed them into envelopes, and sealed them. Then he handed one to Sophia and one to Sarah. "I want you to take these to your parents," he said sternly. "Then I want you both back in this office on Friday, *with your parents*, at four o'clock sharp!"

"Yes, sir," whispered Sarah and Sophia together.

"And Elizabeth," Mr. Clark said with a frown, "innocent or guilty, I don't want to see you in this office again. Understand?"

Elizabeth nodded, too stung to reply. It was so unfair. All she had done was try to get the two girls to work together peacefully. And now she was standing in the principal's office being yelled at for something she had nothing to do with.

In the back of her mind she could hear Jessica's voice, whispering, "I told you so."

"Oh, shut up," Elizabeth muttered under her breath.

Five

$\diamondsuit$

By the time Sophia got the paint scrubbed out of her hair and off of her skin, it was late afternoon. She had left her clothes on top of some newspapers in the kitchen so she wouldn't get paint on any of the furniture. Then she had gotten into the shower with a sponge and the biggest bar of soap she could find.

It took forever to get all the paint off, but finally she felt clean. She stepped out of the shower and put on a pair of sweatpants and a flannel shirt.

As she walked out of the bathroom with a towel wrapped around her hair, she heard the kitchen door slam shut.

"Tony?" Sophia called out.

"It's me," he answered from the kitchen. "What's with these clothes?"

Sophia went into the kitchen and saw Tony examining her paint-splattered clothes with interest.

"I—um—had a paint fight at school," Sophia said in a sheepish tone.

"You what?" Tony said, trying not to laugh.

"A paint fight. Me and this wimpy little crybaby named Sarah Thomas got into a fight in art class. We, uh, we pretty much destroyed one of the art rooms," she explained shakily. "And—oh, Tony," she wailed, "we painted a *teacher*!"

Tony stared at her. "Are you kidding me?" he demanded. "*You* painted a teacher? Sophia Rizzo, my own sister? Sophia Rizzo, the A student? Sophia Rizzo, the overachiever? *You* are in trouble? This is a switch. I thought *I* was supposed to be the one who got into trouble."

"Don't tease me," Sophia begged. "This is really serious, Tony. Mr. Clark sent me home with a note to Mama. He wants to see us both in his office on Friday afternoon."

Tony's face was suddenly grave. "You're right, this is serious, Soph. Mama's going to be pretty upset. Things have been going so well lately with her new job and everything. Now you have to go and blow it by getting yourself into trouble."

"Do you think they can send me to reform school for this?" Sophia asked miserably.

Tony looked at Sophia for a long moment. Then he frowned and nodded his head. "I'm afraid so, Sophia. You know, I've been to reform school twice. I know how the system works. Believe me, painting a teacher will get you a good three years, at least."

Sophia's eyes grew large with fright. "Is it really awful in reform school?" she whispered.

"Not if you know how to fight," Tony said breezily. "I can show you some good defensive moves if you want. Of course, they aren't much good if you get jumped from behind. So you've got to keep your eyes open all the time. Stay out in the open. Always know who's walking behind you. It's just common sense, really."

Sophia's heart was pounding. *I'm finished*, she thought desperately. *People think I'm tough because Tony is. But I'm not. I won't last ten minutes in reform school.*

"And I can get some decent food in to you if you really need me to," he offered.

"Don't they have good food there?" Sophia asked fearfully.

"Oh, sure—if you like bread and water. And sometimes on Sunday, they give you a few pork rinds to round out the meal."

Sophia dropped her head into her hands.

"Don't worry," Tony reassured her. "I can always smuggle some candy bars in to you."

"Oh, great," Sophia wailed. "Not only will I have two black eyes, but I'll be fat, too!"

"That's good," Tony told her. "You want to carry a little extra weight in the joint. It puts more oomph behind your punch."

Sophia turned her horrified eyes on Tony. When she did, she saw the smile lurking around the corners of his mouth.

"Tony Rizzo, I hate you!" she yelled. She pulled the towel off her head and threw it at her brother. "None of this is true. You're just teasing me!"

Tony laughed so hard he fell out of his chair. "Ouch," he managed to say between guffaws.

"Serves you right," Sophia grumbled, trying not to laugh herself. "How could you tell me all those terrible things?"

Tony stood up and ruffled Sophia's wet hair. "Cheer up, sis. You're not going to reform school. Not an ace student like you. You may do a little detention. And Mama's not going to be pleased. But I'm sure everything's going to turn out all right."

Tony was right about one thing. Mrs. Rizzo definitely was not pleased.

"Why you do this?" she demanded that night in her halting English. "We have so much trouble in this family for so long. Now, just when things are better, you do something silly with some painting. What's the matter with you, Sophia?"

Sophia felt sick with shame. Her mother had enough to worry about without Sophia acting like a troublemaker.

When Mr. Rizzo had walked out on his family two years before, he had left behind nothing but a pile of debts and a lot of bitter memories. The family had gone through a terrible time. Tony's anger at the situation had taken the form of stealing cars and fighting in the schoolyard. For a while it had seemed as if the police were at the Rizzos' house almost every other day. But finally, it looked as if things were starting to improve.

Tony's last visit to the juvenile detention center had turned him around. And after a long search for a job, Mrs. Rizzo had finally found work at a company that imported leather handbags from Italy. She loved her work, and she enjoyed talking to the Italian manufacturing representatives. But she also had to deal with buyers from department stores all over the United States. That meant she was under a lot of pressure to improve her English, so she tried to speak English at home as much as possible.

"I'm sorry, Mama," Sophia said, tears welling up in her eyes. "I don't know why I did it. I was just so angry with that girl, Sarah. She's awful. If you met her, you'd understand why I had to do it."

"I don't care what Sarah say to you," Mrs. Rizzo shouted. "Nobody can make you act like that but you. Be careful, Sophia. Don't be like your papa. He was always so angry. So angry he is always picking fights and getting fired. So angry at everybody and everything he runs away and leaves us. You know better than this, Sophia. You know better!"

Sophia wished she could just disappear. She knew how much her mother depended on her to do well in school and act responsibly. Now she had let her mother down.

"You're grounded, Sophia. Grounded is the word, yes? You don't go out until I say you can go. Understand?"

"I understand, Mama," Sophia said with a sob. Then she ran into her room and shut the door.

"It's all Sarah's fault," she sobbed into her pillow. "She's so mean and snobby. It's all her fault!"

Sarah sat in the Thomases' large living room waiting for her father to get home from work. In the kitchen, she could hear Mrs. Donaldson preparing their dinner.

Mrs. Donaldson was the housekeeper Sarah's father had hired to come in the afternoons and evenings. She was there every afternoon when Sarah got home from school, and she never left until Mr. Thomas came home. Somehow, after her mother's death, Sarah couldn't bear to be in their spacious two-story house by herself. The house seemed gloomy and scary when she was there alone—full of creaks and bumps that made her skin crawl.

The only time Sarah had stayed in the house alone was when her father had been dating a woman named Annie. Sarah hadn't liked Annie very much, and Annie had liked Sarah even less. She was mean and sarcastic to Sarah whenever Mr. Thomas wasn't around. Sarah hadn't told her father because she hadn't wanted to make him unhappy.

Then Mr. Thomas had had to go out of town on a sudden business trip. Annie was supposed to come and stay with Sarah while he was away. Instead, she went off and stayed with some of her own friends. She had told Sarah not to tell her father when he called so that he wouldn't worry. So whenever Mr. Thomas had called, Sarah had said that Annie was in the shower or at the grocery store.

Sarah had stayed alone for three days and nights. She was so nervous that she hadn't gotten a wink of sleep, and by the fourth night she had been so exhausted and weak that she had fallen down the steps and been badly injured. If Elizabeth and her family hadn't come looking for Sarah, she might not have lived.

Mr. Thomas had been furious with Annie when he found out. That had been the end of Annie. Shortly afterward, Mr. Thomas had hired Mrs. Donaldson.

Since then, Mr. Thomas and Sarah had spent almost every weekend together. That was exactly the way Sarah liked it. Her father was the most important person in her life, and Sarah was the most important person in his life.

She knew that he was going to be furious when he read Mr. Clark's note. Not furious with Sarah. Furious with Mr. Clark, Sophia Rizzo, and the whole Sweet Valley school system. They had no business forcing a girl like Sarah to associate with somebody like Sophia Rizzo.

Sarah jumped up when she heard her father at the front door. "Daddy!" she cried happily, running to meet him.

Mr. Thomas put down his briefcase and gave Sarah a big hug. "How's my little girl?" he asked.

"Not so hot," Sarah replied in a pouty voice. "I had a terrible day at school, and it wasn't my fault."

Mr. Thomas wrinkled his brow in concern. "What happened, honey?"

"Mr. Sweeney, the art teacher, made me work on a project with this awful girl named Sophia Rizzo. We got into an argument and—well, read this." Sarah handed Mr. Clark's note to her father.

Mr. Thomas sat down in his favorite chair and opened the note. As he read, his frown deepened. Sarah sat quietly and waited for him to finish.

Mr. Thomas folded the note and put it aside. Instead of the sympathetic smile Sarah expected, his expression was stern. "All right, young lady. What do you have to say for yourself?"

"Daddy!" Sarah cried. "You're not mad at *me*, are you? It wasn't my fault."

"According to this note," Mr. Thomas said, "you got involved in a silly squabble with another student and did a fair amount of damage to school property."

Sarah's lip began to tremble. "You're supposed to be on my side," she protested.

"I'm always on your side, Sarah. But this kind of behavior is inexcusable under any circumstances. I shouldn't have to tell you that."

"Excuse me," Mrs. Donaldson said as she stepped into the living room. "Dinner is ready whenever you are."

"We'll talk about this some more after dinner," Mr. Thomas said, still looking stern.

Sarah gave an experimental sniffle, carefully watching her father's face for signs of weakening. Tears, she had discovered, could almost always twist her father around her little finger.

Sarah felt a sob rising in her throat. "I don't want any dinner," she managed to say.

"That's fine," Mr. Thomas said. "But if you'll excuse me, I'm hungry."

Stunned, Sarah watched her father turn his back and walk into the adjoining dining room. Was he really just going to sit and eat his dinner when she was *crying*? Impossible!

"Boo *hoooooo*!" she sobbed as loudly as possible. Mrs. Donaldson looked nervously from Sarah to Mr. Thomas. Mr. Thomas, however, didn't appear to notice anything. He calmly took his seat at the table and put his napkin in his lap.

"Oh, and Sarah," he added. "You're grounded until further notice."

Sarah couldn't stand it anymore. She ran up to her room, slammed the door, and threw herself facedown on the bed.

"He doesn't love me anymore," she sobbed to her teddy bear. "My own father hates me—and it's all Sophia Rizzo's fault!"

Six

◆

Wow, Sophia thought, as she sat with her mother in the waiting room outside Mr. Clark's office. *Mama looks as if she's even more nervous than I am.*

Mrs. Rizzo sat on the edge of her seat, twisting the rings on her fingers around and around. Her dark eyes were large and round as she anxiously watched Mr. Clark's door for signs of movement.

Nevertheless, Sophia was proud of her mother. Her English might not be perfect, and her income might be small, but she looked stylish and elegant. She didn't look like somebody who could be pushed around or bullied. *We Rizzos hang tough*, Sophia thought proudly.

The hall door opened, and Sarah Thomas came in with her father, her hand held firmly in his. *He looks nice*, Sophia thought. Then she looked at Sarah. *I'll bet he spoils her to death*, she added bitterly.

Mr Thomas must have noticed Sophia staring at him, because he gave her a warm smile. "I'm Mr. Thomas," he said, politely extending his hand. "You must be Sophia."

"Yes," Sophia answered, taking his hand. He had a nice handshake—firm and friendly. "This is my mother, Maria Rizzo."

Mrs. Rizzo shook Mr. Thomas's hand and smiled nervously. "This is not such a nice way to meet," she said.

"I can think of lots of places I'd rather be right now," he answered with a chuckle. "Being in the principal's office makes me feel as if I'm in trouble myself."

"It is the same for me," Mrs. Rizzo said, laughing.

Just then the secretary emerged from Mr. Clark's office. "You can go in now," she announced in a cold voice.

Mrs. Rizzo immediately looked nervous again as she stood up. Then she lifted her chin and beckoned to Sophia to follow her. She led the way into Mr. Clark's office with Sarah and Mr. Thomas close behind.

Mr. Clark invited them all to sit down, then eyed the group sternly. "I sent notes home with both girls," he said to Mr. Thomas and Mrs.

Rizzo. "So I know you have some idea of what happened here last Tuesday. Now I'd like to fill you in on the details."

He took a deep breath and launched into the story. Sophia squirmed in her seat. Up until now, the actual event in the art studio hadn't seemed like a very big deal. But as told in Mr. Clark's dry and humorless voice, the story sounded just terrible. *Good grief!* Sophia thought. *He makes it sound as if we robbed a bank at gunpoint or something.*

Mrs. Rizzo sat forward in her seat, listening intently and trying to follow Mr. Clark's rapid-fire English. Sophia could tell her mother wasn't understanding very much. Maybe it was just as well. She was upset enough already.

"Please," Mrs. Rizzo said finally. "I cannot understand. Could you please tell me again, more slowly?"

Mr. Clark looked impatient, but he started over from the beginning. Mrs. Rizzo still looked bewildered and shook her head in frustration.

"Excuse me," Mr. Thomas interrupted. "Perhaps I can help." Then, to Sophia's amazement, Mr. Thomas turned to Mrs. Rizzo and began to tell her the story in flawless Italian.

Sophia's Italian wasn't as good as either her mother's or Mr. Thomas's, but she was able to understand everything he said. In his gentle and good-humored voice, the story didn't sound nearly as bad. In fact, it was kind of funny. At one point, Mrs. Rizzo had to stifle a giggle.

"I understand everything," she said finally. She gave Mr. Clark an apologetic look. "I am very sorry Sophia behaved badly."

Mr. Clark handed Mr. Thomas and Mrs. Rizzo a sheet of paper. "These are the figures on the damage," he said. "As you can see, it's quite extensive."

Mr. Thomas reached into his pocket and pulled out his checkbook. "I'll write you a check for the total right now," he offered.

Mr. Big Shot, Sophia thought sourly. *Trying to buy his way out of trouble.*

"No, no," Mrs. Rizzo protested, pulling her own checkbook from her purse. "That is not fair. I will pay half."

Good for you, Mama, Sophia thought.

"That's not at all necessary," Mr. Thomas said. "Please don't worry about it."

"I insist on paying half," Mrs. Rizzo announced firmly.

Mr. Clark silenced them both with a curt wave of his hand. "Money is not the issue here," he told them sternly. "The school's insurance policy will pay for the damage to the room. It will also compensate Mr. Sweeney for his clothing. The important issue is making the girls responsible for the consequences of their actions."

Mr. Thomas nodded. "I agree. But what do you suggest?"

Mr. Clark cleared his throat and glared at the girls. "I can arrange to have the maintenance staff repaint the art studio next week. But first, the walls and surfaces have to be washed and sanded. I want the girls to do that work on Saturday morning. I want them to do it *together*. Then, they are going to start over on their mural. They will work on it *together*, along with Elizabeth Wakefield, until it is finished."

"That is good," Mrs. Rizzo said. "The punishment will fit the crime."

Mr. Clark rose. "Let me just finish this meeting by saying that if anything like this happens again, I will be forced to take sterner measures."

"It won't happen again," Sophia said softly.

"Sarah?" her father prompted.

"It won't happen again," echoed Sarah.

"Good," Mr. Clark said. "I will see you two here tomorrow morning at eight thirty AM—*together*!"

Mrs. Rizzo and Sophia scurried out of Mr. Clark's office with Sarah and Mr. Thomas close on their heels. As soon as Mr. Clark's door slammed shut behind them, the grown-ups broke out in giggles.

Sophia watched her mother in amazement. Whenever Tony got in trouble, she was upset for days. Now, she hardly seemed angry at all. In fact, she looked prettier than Sophia had seen her look in ages. Her eyes were sparkling with mischief, and her cheeks were glowing.

Mrs. Rizzo brushed her thick curls back from her forehead. "I think maybe things are not so bad after all. Sophia and Sarah will clean the room, and then Mr. Clark will forgive them."

"I think he will," Mr. Thomas agreed. "But you girls had better do a good job. I don't want to have to go through this again."

Even though he had been talking to her and Sarah, Sophia noticed Mr. Thomas never took his eyes off of her mother. "How about some pizza?" he suggested. "I think we could all use some nourishment after our ordeal."

Sophia frowned. Her mother wasn't really going to fall for Mr. Thomas's phoney-baloney charm, was she?

"Fine," Mrs. Rizzo said, smiling shyly.

Apparently, she was.

Half an hour later, Sophia and her mother were sitting across from Sarah and her father at Sweet Valley's poshest pizza restaurant. Red-checkered tablecloths covered the tables and several ferns hung from the ceiling.

Talk about yuppie! Sophia thought scornfully. In her book, ferns did not belong in a serious pizza restaurant. Mrs. Rizzo, on the other hand, seemed delighted with the place.

"It is very pretty in here," she said with a smile. "It reminds me of places in Italy. Tell me, Mr. Thomas, how did you learn to speak Italian so beautifully?"

"I used to travel to Italy frequently on business," he explained.

Soon, he and Mrs. Rizzo were talking like old friends, comparing notes and reminding each other of places they had visited.

Sophia noticed that Sarah was studying the napkin in her lap and carefully avoiding Sophia's eyes. *I don't like this any more than you do*, Sophia thought. *So don't you worry. We're just going to eat our pizza and then get out of your lives.*

Mr. Thomas, though, seemed to have other plans. "Do you like baseball?" Sophia heard him ask, as he and her mother were splitting the last piece of pizza.

"I love baseball," Mrs. Rizzo replied.

"Great. I'll get tickets for the game tomorrow afternoon. The girls will enjoy the fresh air after their hard work. I'll get a ticket for your son, too. Tell me his name again."

"Tony." Mrs. Rizzo smiled. "And he will love to go."

"Hold it," Sophia cried out. "Aren't I grounded?" Sophia loved baseball, but there wa no way she was going to spend any more time with Sarah Thomas than she absolutely had to.

"I'm grounded, too," Sarah spoke up, glaring at Sophia through narrowed eyes.

Mr. Thomas leaned over to Mrs. Rizzo and whispered something in her ear. Mrs. Rizzo whispered something back.

"You two are officially no longer grounded," Mr. Thomas announced with a grin.

Then he and Mrs. Rizzo seemed to forget all about the girls as they chattered away in Italian.

Sophia caught Sarah's eye and pretended to drop her napkin under the table. She jerked her head, signaling Sarah to do the same. Sarah knocked her own napkin onto the floor.

Sophia bent down and ducked her head under the tablecloth. Sarah's angry face peered at her underneath the table. "I'd rather be grounded than go to a baseball game with you," Sophia hissed.

"That goes double for me," Sarah hissed back. Then her face disappeared.

Sophia sat up in her seat and saw Sarah looking cool and composed. Sarah took a small, lady-like bite of pizza. Then she daintily wiped her lips.

Sophia picked up her own slice of pizza and tore off a big bite. When she was sure their parents weren't looking, she chewed it with her mouth wide open, making sure the view for Sarah was as unpleasant as possible.

Sarah pursed her lips. Then she dropped her napkin again and signaled for Sophia to do the same.

Once again, Sophia ducked under the table. "What do you want?" she demanded in a whisper.

"I wanted to tell you that you look even uglier upside down than you do right-side up," Sarah hissed. And then her angry face disappeared again from beneath the table.

Seven

By midmorning on Saturday, Sarah was exhausted. She had spent all morning scrubbing and sanding the art studio and it was still a mess. Worst of all, she was stuck there with nobody to talk to but Sophia Rizzo, the thug.

Actually, she was stuck in the art studio with nobody *not* to talk to but Sophia Rizzo, the thug.

All morning Sarah had maintained a stony and determined silence. Mr. Clark might be able to force her and Sophia to work together, but he couldn't force them to be friends. *I won't say a word to her all day*, Sarah had resolved. *I won't say a word to anybody all day. That will show them how I feel.*

Unfortunately, Sophia seemed just as determined not to talk to Sarah. She hadn't said one word all morning either. Once or twice she had given Sarah a dirty look. And Sarah had given her a dirty look right back.

Sarah stared resentfully at Sophia's back. *I've got my eye on you, Sophia Rizzo*, she thought. *You make one wrong move, and I'll tell my daddy.*

In fact, Sarah almost hoped that Sophia *would* start a fight. Maybe then Mr. Thomas would believe what she had told him about the Rizzos.

Sarah bit her lip, fighting back tears as she remembered the conversation she and her father had had the night before. Sarah had been furious with Mr. Thomas for making plans with the Rizzos. He hadn't considered her feelings at all. He knew how Sarah felt about Sophia and her family, and he had just gone ahead and invited them to the game anyway.

When Sarah had told him about their shabby house and Tony's terrible reputation, she had expected him to call up Mrs. Rizzo and cancel the whole thing right away, but he hadn't. In fact, he had just looked disappointed in her. Then he had given her a long lecture on not judging by appearances.

"You have to learn to see the best in people, Sarah," he had said. "Tony may have gotten himself into some trouble in the past. Lots of young men get into trouble. I got into some trouble myself when I was his age. He probably just needs a little time and encouragement."

"But, Daddy . . ." she had cried.

"And as for their house," he had continued in a firm voice. "Never judge a person by the size of his or her house. Judge him or her by the size of his or her heart and the size of his or her dreams."

Sarah sighed. It was hopeless. Her father obviously had a crush on Mrs. Rizzo, so he was determined to see what he wanted to see. It looked as if it were going to be another Annie episode all over again. Mr. Thomas just couldn't see that Mrs. Rizzo was a grown-up version of Sophia—a no-good, trouble-making bully.

Mr. Thomas had laughed when Sarah had said that about Mrs. Rizzo. Actually, Sarah didn't really believe it herself. If it weren't for the fact that she was Sophia's mother, Sarah might even like Mrs. Rizzo. Sarah couldn't help but admire the way Mrs. Rizzo dressed. She obviously had good taste. Sometimes Sarah missed having a woman to talk to about those kinds of things.

Sarah watched Sophia as she rolled up her sleeves and began to scrub a tabletop. It was hard to believe that she and Mrs. Rizzo were mother and daughter. As usual, Sophia looked sloppy and unkempt. If they had been friends, Sarah would have suggested that Sophia try wearing her hair up in a loose knot. And those baggy sweatshirts definitely had to go. It was too bad Sophia was determined to look like a thug—she was actually kind of pretty.

Sophia looked up at Sarah. She jutted out her chin and defiantly wiped her hands on her sweatshirt. Sarah flinched. Why did Sophia always have to be so crude? Well, if Sophia Rizzo thought she was going to get a response from Sarah, she was wasting her time.

Sarah began furiously scrubbing the tabletop with sandpaper. *I just wish I could do this to Sophia's ugly face!* she thought spitefully.

The harder Sarah scrubbed, the angrier she felt. And the angrier she felt, the harder she scrubbed. She scrubbed the tabletop, the walls, and the floor, until there wasn't anything left to scrub.

Much to Sarah's surprise, the job was finished. She looked at the clock and saw that it was almost noon. Where had the time gone?

Let her sit there like a bump on a log, Sophia thought. *I'll show her! The more fun I have, the more miserable she'll be.* Sophia stood up and cheered as the batter slid into third. Then she put her fingers to her lips and whistled loudly.

It was the bottom of the second inning and the Dodgers were one run behind. Mr. Thomas had gotten terrific seats and it was a beautiful day. Sophia had already polished off two hot dogs and two sodas, and if it weren't for the fact that Sarah Thomas was sitting right next to her, she might have said this was one of the happiest days of her life.

Sophia wasn't sure whose bright idea the seating arrangement had been. Much to her disgust, she found herself sitting between Sarah and her father. Mrs. Rizzo and Tony were on the other side of Mr. Thomas. Sophia leaned forward and looked down the row. She had to smile when she saw her mother's face. Mrs. Rizzo looked beautiful and happy. Even Tony had gone out of his way to look nice for their outing.

There wasn't much extra money in the Rizzo household. A baseball game complete with plenty of hot dogs and peanuts was a real occasion—especially after a morning of hard work.

Sophia had expected to have to do most of the work cleaning up the art studio, but Sarah had surprised her. Sophia hated to admit it, but Sarah had really buckled down and done her share. Of course, she had also given Sophia the silent treatment along with it. *Who cares*, Sophia thought angrily. *I can't stand her whiny little voice anyway.*

Suddenly, Sophia's thoughts were interrupted by a loud "crack." Immediately, her eyes were drawn to the field. The batter began to run as the ball sailed toward the outfield in a smooth arc.

As the ball began its downward curve, the

outfielder positioned himself for the catch. His glove reached upward, ready to snatch the ball out of the sky.

The ball began to fall faster as it neared the ground. The outfielder leaned into the catch, turned slightly—and missed!

"*Run*," Sophia heard Tony bellow.

The stadium erupted like a volcano, the crowd screaming and shouting as the batter ran toward first base like a shot. He streaked across the bag as the opposing team scrambled for the ball.

Sophia let out her breath with a loud gasp. "Go!" she yelled, as loudly as she could. "Go!"

The air was electric with excitement. Mr. Thomas grabbed Sophia's hand and pulled her to her feet. "Go for it!" he shouted.

"*Andiamo!*" screamed Mrs. Rizzo, jumping up and down as the outfield fumbled the ball again and the runner rounded second base and headed for third.

"He's going to make it," Sophia shrieked. "He's going to make it!" Mr. Thomas's hand squeezed hers tightly as the runner began making his way toward home plate. Sarah and everything else was forgotten as a feeling of pure joy swept over Sophia.

The runner slid into home, and the crowd

roared. Mr. Thomas gave Sophia's hand one last squeeze and then turned and hugged her mother. Over his shoulder, Sophia could see her mother's eyes shining with excitement. Even Tony was laughing and whistling. His face looked open and happy, so different from the defensive and sullen expression he used to wear.

Mr. Thomas turned back toward Sophia and smiled. His eyes crinkled with kindness and merriment, and Sophia couldn't help but smile back. As she did, she felt a lump rising in her throat. *I'll bet everybody around us thinks we're a family*, she thought. *We look just like a family is supposed to look.*

Then she noticed Sarah. Sarah hadn't moved or cheered. She stared down at her hands, which were neatly folded in her lap. She looked as if she were trying to pretend she wasn't with the rest of them.

What a party pooper! Sophia thought. *I'm glad we're not a family. I wouldn't have her in my family for a million dollars. Who needs her, or her creepy father either! After today, I hope the Thomases will just leave us alone.*

"Do you like fried chicken?" she heard her mother ask. Sophia leaned forward and frantically tried to catch her mother's eye, but her mother ignored her.

"I love it!" Mr. Thomas said.

"Then let's go tomorrow to Secca Lake. I will fry the chicken tonight. We'll take Tony and the girls."

Sarah and Sophia exchanged a horrified look. "No!" they both shouted at once.

Mr. Thomas and Mrs. Rizzo looked at each other and began to laugh. "Well, we finally got a word out of Sarah," Mr. Thomas said with a chuckle.

Sarah clamped her mouth shut, and her face darkened.

Sophia glanced over at Sarah's sullen face and decided she couldn't stand it anymore. She stealthily reached toward Sarah, grabbed her arm, and pinched it as hard as she could.

"OUCH!" shrieked Sarah. Mrs. Rizzo and Mr. Thomas both looked over at the girls. But by the time they did, Sophia's arms were crossed over her chest and she was staring at the field with an innocent expression on her face.

"Make that two words from Sarah." Mr. Thomas laughed.

"Daddy . . ." Sarah began tearfully.

"Three words," Tony put in with a chuckle.

Sophia couldn't help but smile as she stared at the field. "Give it up," she hissed out of the side of her mouth.

The next thing she knew, a pair of determined fingers were clamping down on the fleshy part of her arm.

Sophia gritted her teeth. *You won't get a peep out of me*, she thought. She edged her foot toward Sarah's, found her toe, and then mashed it under her heel.

Sarah let out a little yelp of pain and loosened her grip on Sophia's arm. "You thug!" Sarah whispered angrily.

"Make that five words," Sophia said with a smirk.

Eight

◇

Sophia sat on her bed and massaged her sore ankles. The pinching and kicking war had continued throughout the game—whenever the grownups weren't looking.

The door to her room was open, and Tony stuck his head inside. "What are you doing?" he asked.

"Look at this," Sophia commanded. Tony stepped closer and looked at Sophia's bruised ankle. "Sarah kicked me," she complained.

"Why? What did you do to her?" he asked.

"What makes you think I did anything to her?" Sophia demanded, sounding hurt.

Tony raised his eyebrows. "Because I don't think Sarah Thomas is the kind of girl who would haul off and kick you for no good reason," he answered reasonably.

"What do you know about Sarah Thomas?" Sophia asked grumpily.

"Her old man seems like a pretty good guy. Somebody you could talk to man to man, if you know what I mean."

"No, I don't know what you mean," Sophia snarled. "Are you implying that I would want to talk to somebody 'man to man'? I may not be as feminine as Sarah Thomas, but I'm not a man. I'm a girl."

"Whoaaa!" Tony said. "Don't take my head off. I know you're a girl. And you know *how* I know you're a girl?" he asked in a serious voice.

"How?" Sophia asked, hoping for a compliment.

"Mom told me," he said solemnly.

"Get out!" Sophia yelled.

Tony laughed so hard he had to hold onto the wall for support.

"GET OUT!" Sophia shouted again.

Mrs. Rizzo stuck her head inside the door. "Stop that, Sophia," she commanded. "Stop that yelling. You're so loud. What would Mr. Thomas think if he could hear you now? I want you to behave tomorrow. Understand? And I don't want you to pinch Sarah."

"Mama!" Sophia protested.

"I saw you." Mrs. Rizzo frowned. "I saw you pinching and kicking when you thought I was not looking. No wonder Sarah is so unhappy and quiet all day. You are a mean girl sometimes. Tomorrow, you behave yourself, or else."

Mrs. Rizzo shook her finger at Sophia. Then she shook it at Tony. "And you, too."

"Wow." Tony grinned as he watched his mother disappear down the hall. "I think she really likes Mr. Thomas. Maybe it wouldn't be such a bad thing if they wound up getting together. Married, even."

Tony ambled off and left Sophia feeling as if she'd just been punched in the stomach. Married! In her wildest dreams, Sophia hadn't considered that possibility. She shut her eyes tightly. "No!" she said firmly. "It can't happen. I won't let it happen. I'll never let my mother marry Sarah Thomas's crummy father."

But no matter how hard she tried, Sophia couldn't stop the fantasy that was forming in her imagination. A fantasy in which Mrs. Rizzo was married to Mr. Thomas, and Sarah Thomas was Sophia's sister. A fantasy in which everybody was happy except for Sophia.

Sophia lay on her bed and let her imagination take over. . . .

"Oh, Sis," Tony called out.

"I'm in here," Sophia answered from the kitchen.

"Where is my favorite little sister hiding?" he called out again in a teasing voice.

"I'm here in the kitchen," Sophia called back. "And I'm not hiding." She was on her hands and knees scrubbing the kitchen floor. She had been there all morning.

Tony came breezing in wearing a brand-new pair of white tennis shorts and tennis shoes. An expensive white sweater was tied around his shoulders and he was swinging a tennis racket. When he saw Sophia, his face fell. "Oh, it's you."

"Aren't I your little sister?" Sophia asked sadly.

"Yes. But you're not my *favorite* little sister. My favorite little sister is Sarah. She's so pretty and feminine. Oh, look, here she is now."

Sarah twirled into the room wearing a pink tutu and carrying a wand. "I'm home from my ballet lesson," she said in a whispery voice.

"Wonderful!" Tony cried. "I've been waiting for you all morning. I wanted to play tennis."

"I would have played tennis with you," Sophia said.

Tony and Sarah looked at each other and laughed. "Can you imagine Sophia playing tennis? She's so clumsy and unrefined!"

Just then Mrs. Rizzo and Mr. Thomas came sweeping into the kitchen holding hands. They were dressed in evening clothes.

"Hello, Sarah darling," Mrs. Rizzo said with a smile. "You look so pretty. I'm sure you're the most talented dancer in your class."

"Yes." Sarah smiled. "I am."

"Then you must come with us tonight. We have two extra tickets to the ball. You and Tony can both come."

"Excellent," Tony said. "Let me just run upstairs and put on my dinner jacket."

"What about me?" Sophia asked mournfully.

Mr. Thomas gave Sophia a haughty look through his monocle. "Please don't snivel, Sophia. I do have something for you."

Mr. Thomas reached into his pocket and pulled out a slip of paper. He handed it to Sophia. "It's a coupon for a free tattoo. When I saw it, I thought immediately of you."

"What do you say, Sophia?" her mother asked sternly.

Sophia stared sadly down at the coupon in her hand. A tear trickled down her cheek. "It expired yesterday."

Sarah Thomas sat on her lacy pink bed in her spacious, sunny bedroom waiting for her father to get home. She absentmindedly rubbed the bruises on her arm and tried to think of ways to talk her father out of going to the picnic with the Rizzos the following day.

She could tell her father was really falling for Mrs. Rizzo, and if she didn't do something about it quickly, who knew how bad it could get. Her father and Mrs. Rizzo could even get . . . *married*. It was almost too horrible to think about. But Sarah couldn't help it. Staring out her window, she slipped into an unhappy fantasy. . . .

"Quick, Sarah, hide me," Mr. Thomas begged as he ran into her room and shut the door. His face was white and frightened.

"What's the matter, Daddy?"

"It's Tony. He's after me again. He wants money." Mr. Thomas fumbled with the door, trying to lock it.

"Tony took all the locks off our doors and sold them," Sarah reminded him.

"I'll get under the bed, then," he whispered.

But before he could move, the door burst open. Tony came barging in, snarling and waving a gun. "Hand it over, Pop."

Mr. Thomas reached into his pocket and pulled out a handful of bills. "Take it," he said, his voice quaking with fear.

Tony counted the money. "This ain't enough," he said with a sneer. "I want more."

"I don't have any more," Mr. Thomas said.

Tony grabbed Mr. Thomas by the arm and began to twist it. "Find some more."

Sarah ran over to her piggy bank and smashed it. "Here," she said quickly. "Here's all the money I have."

Tony rushed over to the dresser to count the pile of change, and Sarah and her father ran out of the room.

Downstairs, they found Mrs. Rizzo and Sophia sitting in the living room. They were wearing matching gold lamé outfits and watching TV—six of them at once.

"Where did all those television sets come from?" Mr. Thomas asked.

Sophia and Mrs. Rizzo exchanged glances. Then they began to laugh nastily. "The same place we got twenty-two stereos, fourteen clock radios, ten personal computers, and the poodle," Mrs. Rizzo replied.

A little black poodle raced out of the kitchen and went straight for Mr. Thomas. "Yip," it barked as it tore the fabric of his slacks.

Sarah and Mr. Thomas retreated into the dining room. It was piled high with merchandise. "Daddy," Sarah whispered. "Is all this stuff *stolen*?"

"I'm afraid so," Mr. Thomas said.

Mrs. Rizzo came to the dining room door and stood with her hands on her hips. Sophia stood behind her and smirked. "We'll be pulling another job tonight," Mrs. Rizzo said. "And you two are going to help load the truck."

"But that's illegal," Mr. Thomas protested.

"Tell it to Tony," Mrs. Rizzo said with a sneer. "Oh, and if you're thinking about trying to run away, don't. Tony sold your car this morning."

Mrs. Rizzo and Sophia went back to their television sets, and Sarah began to weep. "Oh, Daddy! Why did you marry her? We were so happy before they moved in. Now we're prisoners in our own home."

Mr. Thomas patted Sarah's shoulder. "I should have listened to you. You tried to warn me, but I wouldn't listen." And with that, Mr. Thomas began to cry, too.

Nine

"I'm serious. I need you to protect me," Sarah told Elizabeth. It was early the next morning, and Sarah had called Elizabeth to beg her to come along on the picnic. "I want a witness in case Sophia tries anything funny. My father won't believe anything I tell him about the Rizzos."

"Sarah," Elizabeth said, trying to stifle a yawn. "It's not exactly flattering to be invited to go on a picnic to be somebody's bodyguard. Besides, you don't need me. If you leave Sophia alone, she'll leave you alone."

Elizabeth had to giggle as she said it. She was beginning to sound just like her mother. Mrs. Wakefield must have said that to Jessica or Elizabeth a million times when they were little.

"I'm sorry," Sarah said. "I didn't mean it that

way. But it would be fun if you came along. And it won't be any fun at all if you don't."

Elizabeth sighed. She really didn't feel like spending the day listening to Sophia and Sarah argue. On the other hand, she didn't feel like spending the day taking telephone messages for Jessica either.

By now, Jessica's Quake-Field Wakefield story was all over school. Every ten minutes the phone would ring and some student would ask Jessica for free baseball tickets. Jessica was now refusing to answer the phone, and Elizabeth was forced to play secretary. Elizabeth had managed to avoid the same kind of persecution by saying truthfully that Jessica knew more about the family history than she did.

"OK," Elizabeth agreed. "I'll go."

"Thank you." Sarah sighed. "It might turn out to be a nice day after all."

Elizabeth hung up the phone and went upstairs to get dressed. As she passed Jessica's room, her sister popped her head out the door.

"Where are you going?" Jessica asked.

"I'm going to Secca Lake with Sarah Thomas," Elizabeth answered.

"Who's going to answer the phone?" Jessica wailed. "I can't do it. And if I let Mom or Dad answer it, somebody might ask them about Quake-

Field Wakefield. They'll find out about the whole stupid story."

"You could always pretend you're me," Elizabeth joked. "We've switched places lots of times. It should be even easier on the phone."

Jessica's eyes lit up. "That's brilliant, Elizabeth. I'd better put my hair in a ponytail like yours."

Elizabeth laughed. "Nobody's going to see how you're wearing your hair over the phone."

"That's true." Jessica giggled. "But it will help me get into my part. Can I borrow your blue sweater, too?"

Elizabeth shook her head. Sometimes she felt as if she were the only sane person in Sweet Valley.

This is awful, Elizabeth thought later that morning as she sat in the backseat of Mr. Thomas's car between Sarah and Sophia. *I must be as crazy as everybody else after all.*

Neither Sarah nor Sophia had said a word since they started. Elizabeth looked from one to the other and shook her head. *I was definitely out of my mind to come on this picnic.*

Tony, Mr. Thomas, and Mrs. Rizzo, on the other hand, had been talking nonstop in the front seat. Tony had been telling Mr. Thomas about the courses he was taking in school and asking him all kinds of questions. What did Mr. Thomas think about the debate team? What did Mr. Thomas think about intramural soccer? If Mr. Thomas had to choose one or the other, which would he choose? Tony and Mr. Thomas really seemed to be enjoying each other's company.

I wonder why everybody still thinks Tony Rizzo is such a tough guy, Elizabeth thought. *He seems really nice. In fact, everybody seems nice—except Sophia and Sarah.*

Finally, they reached the lake, and Mr. Thomas parked the car near the picnic grounds.

"I brought the grill," he told Mrs. Rizzo. "I thought some hot dogs and hamburgers might go well with the fried chicken."

Everyone got out of the car, and Mr. Thomas opened the trunk. They all grabbed something to carry, and Sophia and Sarah both reached for the grill at the same time.

"I'll carry the grill," Sophia said as they lifted it out of the trunk.

Sarah continued to hold onto the handle. "No, *I'll* carry it."

"Suit yourself," Sophia said, letting go.

Sarah hadn't expected the sudden weight, and she dropped the grill.

"DADDY!" she wailed.

Mr. Thomas turned. "What is it?" he asked impatiently.

Sarah hopped up and down. "My toe. I think it's broken."

Elizabeth rolled her eyes. She had seen the grill fall. It had hit the ground at least four inches from Sarah's foot. Why was Sarah trying to create such a fuss?

Mrs. Rizzo looked concerned and started walking in Sarah's direction. But Mr. Thomas took her hand and pulled her gently toward the picnic grounds. "She'll be all right," Elizabeth heard him say.

Sarah's mouth formed a small pouty "oh" when she realized her father wasn't going to come to her aid.

"Let me help you," Sophia offered.

As Elizabeth watched, Sophia picked up the grill. At the same time, she managed to put her foot right in Sarah's path.

"Yikes!" Sarah gasped as she fell face forward on the dusty ground.

Sophia laughed.

"Cut it out, you two," Tony said, as he brushed past them with a bag of charcoal.

Elizabeth closed the trunk of the car and sighed. It was going to be a long day.

* * *

It was a beautiful day at the lake. It was cool and crisp—a perfect day for a picnic.

Sophia was glad Sarah had asked Elizabeth along. It gave her somebody to talk to. "I wish we could have left her at home," Sophia whispered to Elizabeth.

"Why can't you two try to get along?" Elizabeth whispered back.

"Because she's impossible," Sophia said. "Don't you think so?"

"I'm not going to take sides," said Elizabeth. "I'm going to get another hot dog."

When Elizabeth stood up, Sophia noticed that the mat they were sitting on was covered with dirt and sand. A sudden breeze gave her an idea. She giggled as she watched Sarah munching on a hot dog a few feet away.

"Time to shake out this mat," Sophia said in a pleasant voice. She stood, picked up the mat, and gave it a snap. Immediately, dirt and sand blew in Sarah's direction, covering the food on her plate and sticking in her hair.

"DADDY!" Sarah shrieked.

Mr. Thomas was busy with the grill. "What is it?" he shouted.

"Look what she did," Sarah cried. "I've got dirt and sand all over me."

"Just brush yourself off, Sarah. I'm sure it was an accident."

"It wasn't. She did it on purpose."

"Did not!" Sophia insisted, even though she had.

"Did, too!"

Sophia saw Mr. Thomas whisper something to Tony, Mrs. Rizzo, and Elizabeth. The next thing she knew, they all were marching toward Sarah.

"All right, Sarah. We're going to help you get some of that dirt and sand off," her father said.

Sarah's instinct for self-preservation kicked in about two seconds too late. By the time she realized what they were planning, they already had her by the arms and legs.

"ONE . . . TWO . . . THREE . . ." they chanted, as they swung her toward the lake.

And then . . . SPLASH!

Sarah let out an outraged shriek as she hit the water.

The group laughed as they walked back up the bank toward Sophia.

"Way to go!" Sophia shouted, laughing. "She's been asking for it all day."

"She's not the only one," Tony said with a mischievous smile.

Sophia's laughter came to an abrupt halt. "Oh, no . . ." she said, backing up.

"Oh, yes," they all shouted as they reached forward and grabbed her.

"ONE . . . TWO . . . THREE . . ." they chanted again.

And then . . . SPLASH!

The dark, cold water closed over Sophia's head, and she flailed around until her feet found the soft and squishy bottom. When she stood up, she discovered that the water was only waist deep. Sophia wiped the mud from her eyes and spit out a mouthful of swampy water.

"Watch where you're spitting," Sarah said in a cold, threatening voice.

Sophia turned and discovered that Sarah was right next to her. Sarah looked as if she were wearing a seaweed hat, and something slimy was wrapped around Sophia's neck.

Sophia spat again, just to irritate Sarah. Then she scowled. "This is all your fault."

"*My* fault," said Sarah angrily. "How do you figure it's my fault?"

"Well, it's somebody's fault," Sophia insisted. "It's not mine—so it must be yours." Just as she finished her sentence, something slithered past her arm.

Sophia's heart leaped into her throat. "A *snake!*" she screamed. Sophia was more afraid of snakes than anything in the world. Without thinking, she jumped into Sarah's arms for protection.

Sarah immediately dumped her back into the

water and began to giggle. "That was seaweed, dummy."

"Seaweed?" Sophia's heartbeat began to slow.

"Seaweed."

Sophia felt a flush of embarrassment. She peered nervously down into the water. "It *could* have been a snake."

Sarah began to giggle harder. "No, it couldn't. It's the wrong season. Besides, I've never heard of any snakes in Secca Lake." Then she began to really laugh. "I wish you could have seen your face."

Sophia tried not to smile. But looking at Sarah with seaweed on her head was just too funny. Besides, Sarah's laughter was infectious. Soon, Sophia and Sarah were both convulsed in giggles.

Suddenly, the whole situation seemed like the funniest thing in the whole world. The girls fell into each other's arms, laughing and trying to hold each other up as they slid around on the muddy bottom of the lake.

As Sophia gasped for breath, she looked toward the bank. Mr. Thomas and Mrs. Rizzo stood with their backs to them. They were looking off into the trees and they had their arms wrapped around each other's waists.

Suddenly Sophia stopped laughing, and so did Sarah. They looked at each other and scowled.

Sophia took a deep breath. "I think it's time we both got on the same team," she said finally.

"What do you mean?" Sarah asked slowly.

"I mean neither one of us is exactly overjoyed about what's going on between our parents. So why don't we put our heads together and do something about it?"

Sarah pulled a string of seaweed out of her hair. "That's fine with me."

Sophia thrust her hand toward Sarah. "Shake on it?"

Sarah hesitated a moment. Then she took Sophia's hand and shook it firmly. "Let's get out of this stinky water," she said.

As Sophia and Sarah climbed out of the water, they could hear Mr. Thomas's voice drifting toward them. "How about dinner tomorrow night? This time we'll leave the kids at home."

Sophia turned to Sarah. "Hear that? What are we going to do?"

Sarah's face looked grim, and there was a determined note in her soft voice. "When I want something, I usually get it the old-fashioned way."

Sophia gave her a puzzled look. "What are you talking about?"

"Guilt," Sarah said simply.

Ten

◇

On Sunday night, Sarah lay in her bed, determined *not* to fall asleep. She knew from experience that unless she got a good night's sleep, she would wake up with dark circles under her eyes and her pale complexion would look sallow and waxy.

In the months after her mother's death, Sarah had often had trouble sleeping. Bad dreams had kept her awake night after night. Every little thump, bump, or creak frightened her and made her think of monsters, ghosts, and witches. Then she would lie wide awake, shivering under her covers until morning.

Her appearance had worried her father, and he had taken her to the doctor three or four times just to be sure everything was all right. Sometimes, after a really bad night, he would stay home from work so that he could be with her.

Gradually, things had improved. Sarah seldom had trouble sleeping these days. But she still slept with a night-light on, even though she'd die of embarrassment if anybody ever found out about it.

Tomorrow morning, Sarah was determined to look terrible. She would tell her father she couldn't sleep because she was having nightmares again. Nightmares about an evil stepmother—an evil stepmother with evil children.

There was no way Mr. Thomas would go running off to have dinner with Mrs. Rizzo after that. He wouldn't want to see his daughter emotionally scarred for life, would he? It was the perfect plan.

Sarah settled herself more comfortably against her pillows. All she had to do was stay awake . . . stay alert . . . stay . . .

Sarah jerked herself back from the brink of sleep. Maybe this wasn't going to be as easy as she thought.

Sarah thumped her pillows. Then she sat up as straight as possible. She opened her eyes wide. She wouldn't even blink if she could help it.

After a few minutes, the lids of her eyes began to feel very heavy.

This is ridiculous, Sarah thought, shaking herself. *I guess I'm going to have to scare myself. That will keep me awake for sure.* She turned her eyes toward the window. Two long, bony arms were tapping on the glass. They were trying to reach inside and snatch her out of bed. They were going to wrap around her neck and . . .

Sarah sighed. It was useless. They might look like long bony arms, but Sarah knew that they were just a couple of tree branches.

There was a sickening thump from somewhere downstairs . . . and then a slow, ominous creaking.

It's an ax murderer, Sarah thought. *He's broken through the kitchen door, and he's slowly creeping toward the stairs.*

Sarah held her breath. Any minute now, she'd start to hear the footsteps. Footsteps that went "thump . . . thump . . . thump."

Sarah waited. She cocked her head and turned her ear toward the hall. She held her breath. Where were the footsteps?

Suddenly, there was a "whoosh" sound and then a steady "hummmm."

Sarah flopped back impatiently on her pillows. Phooey! It was just the central air-conditioning adjusting itself. Where was the crazed ax murderer when she needed him?

She mentally ran through her list of sure-fire, guaranteed-to-keep-her-awake fears.

There's a vampire in my closet, she thought. Then she giggled. *He must be pretty uncomfortable in there. That closet's packed solid with junk.*

Vampires, obviously, were not going to do the trick.

What about creatures from outer space? Giant insects? Zombies? Mad scientists?

But no matter how hard she tried, Sarah just couldn't work up a good scare. This was a situation that called for drastic action.

Sarah got out of bed, walked over to the night-light, and—turned it off. *That ought to do it*, she thought with a shudder. *I'll be awake all night now.*

Sarah ran back to her bed and jumped in. She looked around the room, waiting for the dark and gloomy shadows to come to life. Any minute now, they would start to loom and threaten.

The cool night seemed to close around her like a soft blanket as her eyelids began to close. . . .

Sarah awoke with a start. It was morning.

"Oh, no!" she gasped. "I've been asleep." She dashed to the mirror and her face fell. "This is awful. I look great."

"Sarah," she heard Mr. Thomas call from downstairs. "Breakfast is ready."

Sarah grabbed her robe and ran down to the kitchen.

Mr. Thomas was already sitting at the table. In front of him was a big plate of pancakes and bacon. He smiled when he saw Sarah's face. "You're looking very pretty this morning."

Sarah frowned. "I don't feel very pretty. I feel awful. I had nightmares all night long."

Mr. Thomas looked skeptical.

"I really did," Sarah insisted. "Nightmares about a wicked stepmother."

Mr. Thomas began to laugh.

Sarah stuck out her lip. Obviously, he wasn't going to respond to hints. Well, she decided, if you can't be subtle, be blunt. "How long do you think you should know someone before you marry them?" she asked.

Mr. Thomas put down his fork and gave Sarah his full attention. "I know what this is about, Sarah. And I can't answer your question. No one can. What I *can* tell you is that Mrs. Rizzo and I aren't rushing into anything. OK?"

Sarah lowered her eyes. "OK," she said reluctantly.

"Darn that Sarah Thomas," Sophia muttered, dashing inside the house and up to the bathroom. She had had to race all the way home from her *Sixers* meeting to make sure she got there before her mother did. *Sarah can't do anything right*, Sophia thought angrily. *She was supposed to sabotage their date and what does she do? She falls asleep. Now it's all up to me.*

Sophia rifled through the bathroom cabinet, located the shampoo, and threw it out the bathroom window.

Then she ran into her mother's bedroom and threw open the closet. She found the silk blouse Mrs. Rizzo always wore on special occasions, pulled it out, and crushed the delicate material between her hands until it was creased and soiled. *No way will she wear that*, Sophia thought with a smile.

Next she turned her attention to the dressing table. She quickly picked up the eye shadow and blush and dropped them on the floor. The colorful cakes of powder shattered, and Sophia threw the pieces into the garbage. If her mother asked what had happened, Sophia would say that the cat had jumped up on the table and broken everything.

Sophia knew how much pride her mother took in her appearance. If Mrs. Rizzo couldn't wash her hair, find anything to wear, or make up her face, she'd probably be too embarrassed to go out. Sophia quickly looked around the room. "I think that's everything," she said out loud. "Now, I just have to sit back and wait."

The telephone began to ring, and Sophia grabbed the receiver. "Hello," she answered breathlessly.

It was her mother. "Sophia, dear, I must work a little late this evening. So I will go from here to meet Mr. Thomas for dinner. There is some pasta and a salad in the refrigerator for you and Tony. All you have to do is heat the pasta."

Sophia sighed. "OK, Mama."

"Good-bye, and I will see you later tonight." Her mother hung up the phone.

Sophia held on to the receiver for a moment. Then she slammed it down. "DARN!"

Eleven

◇

On Tuesday afternoon, Elizabeth raced into art class just as the bell rang. Sophia and Sarah were there already.

When Elizabeth joined them, she saw that Sarah had brought in the new mural sketch. It was even better than the first one.

"Sarah," Elizabeth cried. "This is great. When did you have time to do it?"

"I started last night," Sarah answered. She threw Sophia an angry look. "I worked until my dad got home—and it was *very* late."

Sophia frowned. "Too bad you couldn't manage to stay up on Sunday night. Then you might not have had to stay up last night at all."

"I wouldn't have had to stay up either night if somebody had done what they said they were going to do after school yesterday."

"I couldn't help that," Sophia argued.

Elizabeth groaned. "I don't know what you two are arguing about, and I don't care. All I want to do is get this mural finished."

Just then, Mr. Sweeney came over. Elizabeth watched him carefully. He gave the girls a frosty look. *He may have forgiven*, thought Elizabeth. *But he hasn't forgotten*.

But when Mr. Sweeney saw the mural sketch, he broke into a broad smile. "This is wonderful!" He carefully examined the drawing. "In spite of your—uh—setback, you three are still way ahead of the others. Do you think you could possibly finish it by next week?"

The three girls looked at each other. If they were going to finish by next week, they had to have a place to work. The studio next door was out. It was still being painted. But nobody wanted to bring up that painful subject.

There was an uncomfortable silence until Sarah finally spoke up. "We can use my dad's workroom in the basement," she offered. "He won't mind."

"Super," Mr. Sweeney said happily. He was so busy admiring their work that he seemed to have forgotten all about them. He hummed a little under his breath as he peered down through his glasses. He began to mutter to himself absentmindedly. "Sound ideas . . . nice perspective there in the foreground . . . ah yes, very amusing . . . this is so good it almost makes up for . . ."

Mr. Sweeney suddenly remembered the three girls. He eyed them nervously and cleared his throat. "Ahem!" The smile abruptly disappeared and was replaced by a stern frown. "Carry on, then," he said as he quickly walked away.

The three girls began to giggle.

"Poor Mr. Sweeney," Sophia said, laughing. "I think he's more afraid of us than we are of him."

After school, the three girls carried the sketch to Sarah's house. Sarah introduced Elizabeth and Sophia to Mrs. Donaldson.

Mrs. Donaldson seemed surprised and delighted that Sarah had brought home company. She immediately dropped the vacuum cleaner and hurried into the kitchen to fix the girls a snack.

Sarah showed Elizabeth and Sophia around the house, and then they went back to the kitchen. Mrs. Donaldson's "snack" looked more like a feast. There were stacks of little sandwiches—Elizabeth counted at least three different kinds—dips and potato chips, piles of cookies, cheese straws, little chocolates wrapped in gold foil, cold milk, and sodas.

"Oh, boy!" Sophia exclaimed. "This is some snack."

"This looks wonderful!" Elizabeth said, her mouth watering.

"Is there anything else you girls might like?" Mrs. Donaldson asked anxiously.

"This looks like plenty," Elizabeth said.

"Then please sit down," Mrs. Donaldson urged them.

The girls sat down and dug in with enthusiasm. Soon, they were all eating and talking happily.

Mrs. Donaldson kept bringing fresh supplies of everything to the table. She watched with fond approval as Sarah reached for more sandwiches. "It's nice to see Sarah with an appetite," Mrs. Donaldson said with a laugh. "I usually have to twist her arm to get her to eat."

Suddenly, Elizabeth understood why Mrs. Donaldson seemed so eager to please. *I'll bet Sarah doesn't have much company*, she thought. *Mrs. Donaldson wants to make sure we have a good time so we'll come back. She wants Sarah to have friends.*

With a sudden flash of insight, Elizabeth caught a glimpse of the lonely life Sarah was leading. She wondered if Sarah herself realized how lonely she was.

"Let's go to the basement," Sarah said, when the girls couldn't eat another bite. "My dad has a long worktable down there where we can paint."

She laughed. "This time, let's paint the mural and not each other."

Elizabeth and Sophia laughed, too, and followed Sarah through the door in the kitchen that led to the basement.

They went through a laundry room, and Sarah opened another door. Elizabeth gasped when she stepped through. It was like being inside a paper garden. Beautiful kites of every color and design hung from the walls and ceiling.

"Did your dad make all these?" Sophia asked, her eyes wide with astonishment.

Sarah nodded proudly. "He's been making kites for years. On windy days, he and I always go kite flying."

Sophia's face tightened for a brief moment. She swallowed hard. "That must be nice. Doing things with your dad, I mean."

Elizabeth had another flash of insight. She realized Sophia was lonely, too. *I'm reading everybody's mind today*, she thought, shaking her head.

Sarah set out buckets of paint and handed out brushes. The girls began to work. As they painted, they chatted about school, boys, television shows, music, and a million other things. For the first time, Elizabeth actually enjoyed being with Sarah and Sophia. When they forgot their differences, they were good company.

The time flew by. Before they knew it, the afternoon was over, and Mr. Thomas was home from work. Elizabeth thought he looked very handsome and young as he stood in the basement, talking and laughing with Sarah and Sophia. He thought the drawings were hilarious. Sophia's eyes sparkled as she explained the significance of each and every caricature.

"Hello!" they heard a voice call. Mrs. Rizzo suddenly appeared in the doorway. She wore a royal-blue linen suit and she looked beautiful against the colorful backdrop of the kites.

"It's getting dark, and I did not want Sophia to walk home alone," she explained, smiling at Mr. Thomas.

"I'm glad you're here," Mr. Thomas said, smiling back. "I've been wanting you to see my workshop."

"You made all these beautiful kites yourself?" she asked in surprise. "I love kites. When I was a little girl, I had a kite, and it was my favorite thing in the whole world."

"Really? How big was it?" Mr. Thomas asked.

"About like that," she said, pointing to a large kite hanging from the ceiling. "It was pink and it had a dragon on it."

"Light pink or dark pink?" Mr. Thomas asked.

"Bright pink, like Sarah's blouse." Mrs. Rizzo gave Sarah a warm smile, and Sarah smiled back.

Mr. Thomas went on with his questions. "Was the dragon fierce, or friendly?"

"Oh, very fierce. But friendly to me." She laughed.

"What happened to the kite, Mama?" Sophia asked.

Mrs. Rizzo sighed sadly. "It got caught in a tree. The rain came, and then it was gone."

"Come up and have a cup of coffee while Sophia gets her things together," Mr. Thomas suggested.

Mr. Thomas and Mrs. Rizzo went up the basement stairs, laughing and talking. Sarah and Sophia stared after them in silence.

"Your parents look really cute together," Elizabeth said finally.

Both Sarah and Sophia turned to stare at her. Sarah's face had gone blank, and Sophia's expression was sullen.

"I'll get my things," Sophia muttered. Then she turned to Elizabeth. "We'll give you a ride home if you want. But hurry up and get your stuff together. I don't want them getting too friendly up there."

"Hi," Sarah said to Sophia in a small voice. It was Thursday afternoon, and Sarah had looked all over school for Sophia before finally spotting her by the lockers.

"Hi," Sophia said.

Sarah looked down at her feet. This was going to be harder than she thought.

"Well?" Sophia said in her gruffest voice. "What do you want?"

Sarah reached into her pocket and pulled out an envelope full of photographs. They were old photographs of her father with his former girl-friend, Annie.

"I thought we might be able to use these," Sarah said in a low voice. She was almost whis-pering. There was a sick, ashamed feeling in her stomach.

Sophia frowned as she flipped through the photographs. They had been taken one weekend at the lake. Mr. Thomas had his arm around Annie in most of the shots. In one picture, he was kissing her.

"Your dad really gets around," Sophia said in a hard and angry tone.

"That's his *old* girlfriend," Sarah protested. "He doesn't see her anymore. Honest! He doesn't like her at all, and neither do I."

Sophia gave her a curious look. "Why are you showing these to me?"

Sarah swallowed. "I thought maybe if your mom saw these, she might think what you thought, and . . ." Sarah trailed off. She pictured Mrs. Rizzo crying, and it made her sad. Sarah really liked Mrs. Rizzo. The only thing she didn't like about her was the fact that she was Sophia's mother.

Sophia frowned. "I see what you're getting at. But . . ."

Sarah almost hoped Sophia would refuse to go along. "If you don't want to, that's fine," she said quickly.

"They're your pictures," Sophia said. "It's up to you. Do you want to?"

"Only if you want to," Sarah hedged.

Sophia pursed her lips. "OK," she said finally. "Let's do it. But write something on the back. Write 'He's engaged to me so back off!' "

"Don't you think that's a little strong?" Sarah asked.

"Forget it. Write whatever you want," Sophia shouted.

"Don't shout at me!" Sarah shouted back.

"Then just write it and give me the pictures!" Sophia shouted even louder. "I'll put them in the mailbox for my mom to find tonight. OK?"

"OK!"

"FINE!"

"FINE!"

Twelve

◇

"Why is everybody so quiet?" Tony asked that evening at dinner.

Mrs. Rizzo didn't say anything. Her face was miserable.

"Did you have a bad day at work?" Sophia asked, trying to make her voice sound innocent.

Mrs. Rizzo still didn't say anything. She looked as if she were trying to make up her mind about something. Then, her expression changed from miserable to angry. She threw her napkin down and stood up. She marched to the phone and began dialing.

As she waited for someone to answer, she tapped her foot irritably. When someone on the other end picked up, she launched into a speech in rapid Italian.

Sophia and Tony gaped. Their mother had a

quick temper, but neither of them had ever seen her this angry before. She spoke mostly in Italian, but she switched to English for the big finish. ". . . and I think you are just a *two-timing, double-dealing, kite-flying cad!*"

Mrs. Rizzo slammed the phone down. Then, in front of Sophia's and Tony's horrified eyes, she burst into tears and ran into her bedroom.

Sophia felt awful. She wanted to run after her mother and tell her the whole truth.

Don't be stupid, she told herself sternly. *This is exactly what you wanted.*

The next day at lunch, Sophia took her tray and sat down with Sarah. At first, neither of them said a word. Sarah's face was pale and forlorn.

"It worked," Sarah said in a soft, unhappy voice.

"Looks like it," Sophia agreed.

There was a long silence.

"My father is really angry that your mom didn't give him a chance to explain," Sarah said. "He's sad, too. I heard him pacing in his room all night."

"I don't know why you sound so upset about it," Sophia said. Her voice was impatient. "This is just what we wanted. At least it's what *I* wanted. Maybe you're not as upset about the idea of our parents getting together as I am."

"It's what I wanted, too," Sarah responded belligerently.

Sophia put down her sandwich. She wasn't hungry anymore. "Good. Then I'll see you at your house Sunday afternoon. We're supposed to work on the mural, right?"

Sarah nodded. "Right."

Friday night was grim at the Thomases' household. Mr. Thomas tried his best to act cheerful and normal, but Sarah could tell he was miserable. *He's acting the way he did after Mom died*, Sarah thought. *He's trying to act like everything's going to be all right. But it's just an act. He's only doing it for my sake.*

Saturday was just as bad. Mr. Thomas woke Sarah up early. It was as if he couldn't stand to be in the house. They went shopping and to the movies. They went out to lunch, and they went out to dinner. They went for a drive, and they went for a walk. Mr. Thomas kept them busy every single minute.

It was late when they got home. Sarah was tired, but Mr. Thomas was still restless. Finally, he put on a jacket and sat by himself in the backyard, staring at the sky.

This is awful, Sarah thought.

Instinctively, she reached for the phone and called Sophia.

"Hello," Sophia answered.

"It's me," Sarah said in a soft voice. "How's it going at your house?"

"My mom's been really unhappy all day," Sophia replied. "She cleaned the house—twice. Then she replanted all the window boxes, even though they didn't need replanting at all. Then she cleaned the house again."

"I guess she's trying to keep busy," Sarah said. "My dad's been doing the same thing." She took a deep breath. "Did we do the right thing?"

There was a long pause.

"Absolutely!" Sophia finally said, a little too forcefully. "I don't want my mother getting hurt. She doesn't need another man walking out on her. So it's better that they break up now. It's for their own good. Your dad doesn't need another bad experience either."

"You're right," Sarah agreed. "He doesn't. I don't ever want to see him get hurt again the way Annie hurt him—not that your mom is anything like Annie."

"And I didn't mean that your father was anything like my dad," Sophia said anxiously.

"I know," Sarah said. "So what else is going on with you?"

Sarah and Sophia talked on the phone for another half hour. Sarah told Sophia about the comedy movie she had seen with her father. They both laughed as Sarah described the silly car chases and the ridiculous costumes.

When Sarah hung up, she felt pretty cheerful. It was funny how talking to Sophia seemed to make her feel so much better. It was almost as if they were friends!

On Sunday, Sarah woke up early. She wanted to get all her homework finished so she could have the afternoon free to work on the mural.

When she went down to the kitchen for some juice, her father was already up and drinking coffee.

"You're up," he said happily. "That's great. Throw on some clothes, and let's go out for breakfast."

Sarah really needed the time to study, but she hated to let him down. After all, he was going through a bad time.

They went to a local diner and her father ordered a huge stack of pancakes. Halfway through, he seemed to lose his appetite.

Suddenly, Sarah seemed to lose hers, too.

Mr. Thomas put some money on the table. "Let's go to the zoo," he said.

After the zoo, they went to the hardware store. Mr. Thomas seemed determined to examine every single item. Sarah sighed impatiently. Weren't they ever going home?

Sarah looked at her watch. It was almost one thirty. "Dad," she said. "We need to go home. I have some friends coming over at two o'clock."

"You do?" Mr. Thomas blinked in surprise. Then he seemed to realize that probably didn't sound very flattering to Sarah. "Uh—sure. Of course you do," he added quickly. Sarah almost giggled.

He quickly paid for a screwdriver and they went out to the car.

"Maybe we can do something together tonight," Sarah said, feeling a little guilty.

"That would be great," Mr. Thomas said.

It's like we've switched places, Sarah thought. *I'm worrying about keeping* him *company now.*

They got to the house minutes before Sophia and Elizabeth arrived. Mr. Thomas said hello to the girls and then disappeared into his study.

"How's he doing?" Sophia asked in a low tone.

"Not too well," Sarah answered.

"What's the matter?" Elizabeth asked. "Is he sick?"

Sarah and Sophia exchanged glances.

"No," Sarah answered. "But we finally came up with a way to break up our parents. So they're both going through a bad time."

Together Sarah and Sophia explained to Elizabeth what they had done.

Elizabeth shook her head in disbelief. "I hope you two know what you're doing."

There was an uncomfortable silence. "So, did you do any more work on the mural?" Elizabeth asked Sarah.

"No," Sarah said. "I haven't had time. Besides, my dad was using his workshop Thursday and Friday nights. Let's get right to work and maybe we can finish today."

Sarah led the way down to the basement workshop. She scurried around, gathering up the brushes and rags. "Look behind those boxes and see if there's a bucket," she told Sophia.

Sophia went over to a crowded corner of the workroom. She moved some large pieces of cardboard aside and gasped. She looked stunned—almost as if she were about to cry. Wordlessly, she reached down and picked up something for the other girls to see.

It was a kite. Or at least it was the beginning of a kite. It had no tail and was only partially painted. But they all knew whose kite it was. It was bright pink with a very fierce dragon.

"Your dad is a really great guy," Sophia whispered, choking back her tears.

Sarah felt a tear running down her own cheek. "So that's what he was working on Thursday and Friday. A kite for your mom."

Sophia placed the delicate kite carefully back

in the corner. She let out a big breath. "We made a mistake," she said.

"A big mistake," Sarah agreed.

"So how are you going to fix it?" Elizabeth asked.

Thirteen

When Elizabeth, Sarah, and Sophia unrolled their mural in art class on Tuesday afternoon, the class broke into enthusiastic applause.

"Good work!" Mr. Sweeney said. "You did a great job with the assignment. Ms. Luster is going to be thrilled." He turned to face the rest of the class. "I hope this will inspire the rest of you to move along. In case I forgot to mention it, I *will* be grading this project. So I want to see finished work by next week."

"Hear that, Jessica?" Ken said. He, Jessica, and Lloyd were sitting together at a table in the corner. "We're supposed to be finished by next week, and we've hardly even started. It would be a lot easier if you would call Quake-Field."

"You guys are the two most stubborn people in the whole world," Jessica said. "I've told you a hundred times I'm not calling him. So why don't we just give up on this stupid baseball thing? I never even liked the idea to begin with."

"All in favor of sticking with the baseball idea, say 'aye,' " Lloyd said seriously.

"Aye," he and Ken said together. Jessica rolled her eyes.

"All opposed?" Lloyd asked.

"Make that opposed with a capital O," Jessica said with a frown.

"It's two against one," Ken said happily. "You're out-voted. So when are you going to call him?"

"*Never*," Jessica said. "If you want to draw a picture of him, you'll just have to copy it from a magazine or something."

"We've tried," Lloyd exclaimed. He opened his notebook and handed Jessica some sketches. "We just can't seem to make it look like him."

Jessica laughed. "This doesn't look like anybody. Anybody human, that is." The sketches really were hilarious. In some of them, Quake-Field resembled a fire hydrant. In others, he looked like a lamppost.

"It would be a lot easier if we could get him to pose," Ken said.

"That's impossible," Jessica insisted.

Ken and Lloyd exchanged a smile.

"Maybe not," Ken said.

Jessica looked at them suspiciously. "You guys are up to something. What is it?"

"You'll only hear about it if it works," Ken said.

Meanwhile, Elizabeth, Sarah, and Sophia had gone to the library to hang up their mural. Mr. Sweeney had been right. Ms. Luster was thrilled with the mural. "It's attractive and it makes a wonderful statement about the importance of recycling," Ms. Luster said excitedly when the girls hung their mural in the library. "You girls make a great team. I hope all your projects are this successful."

Sarah and Sophia grinned at each other. "We hope so, too," Sophia said.

As soon as Ms. Luster left the room, Sophia and Sarah began to talk excitedly.

"I told Tony what we did," Sophia said. "He was really mad at me, but he's going to help us."

"Good," Sarah said. "We're going to need all the help we can get. I've been talking about you nonstop, but my dad still hasn't asked about your mom at all. Sometimes he's really dense."

"No, he's not. Your dad is great," Sophia said. "Look how much time he spends with you. He's always looking out for you. He's just feeling hurt now, that's all. Just be glad you're not at my house. Mama's turned into a mean cleaning machine. All she does is clean the house and snap at me and Tony. She yelled at me for fifteen minutes this morning because she didn't like the blouse I was wearing.''

"You should listen to her. She's got really good taste.''

Sophia looked down at her blouse. "Thanks a lot.''

Sarah giggled. "Seriously. I wish I had a mom to help me with clothes. My father doesn't know anything about that kind of stuff.'' She looked up at Sophia. "So, has your mom said anything about him at all?''

Sophia pushed a thumbtack into place. "No. I've given her a million chances to bring up the subject, but she won't bite. We may have to get more aggressive.''

The way they're plotting and planning, they sound just like me and Jessica, Elizabeth thought with a smile. *You'd think they were sisters.*

"I saw a new kite in the basement,'' Sarah said casually to her father that night.

They were sitting together in the living room, and Mr. Thomas was lost in a book. After trying to bring up the subject of Mrs. Rizzo in several subtle ways and failing, Sarah had decided to take the bull by the horns.

Mr. Thomas grunted from behind his book.

Sarah went on. "A pink one—with a dragon.''

Mr. Thomas said nothing.

"I hope you're going to finish it. It's one of the prettiest ones you've made."

Mr. Thomas turned a page.

"It's important to finish the things you start," she added.

Mr. Thomas lowered his book and gave her a curious look.

Sarah met her father's steady gaze. "That's what you're always telling me. Right?"

Mr. Thomas just sighed and looked away.

After dinner, Sophia went into her mother's bedroom and told her the truth about the pictures.

Much to her surprise, Mrs. Rizzo didn't get angry. But she didn't cheer up, either. She just looked sad and lonely.

"It's for the best," she said quietly. "I'm sure it would not have worked out anyway."

"Call him, Mama."

"No. Not after the things I said. It would be too hard for him to forgive. Let's not talk again about this."

Finally, Sophia went to the telephone and held a whispered conference with Sarah. Then she consulted with Tony.

When their mother came into the kitchen for some hot tea, Sophia nudged Tony under the table with her foot.

"Let's go to the park on Saturday," Tony suggested. "All three of us. We'll have a picnic."

"You go with Sophia," Mrs. Rizzo said. "I have things to do here. Things to clean."

"Mama, the house is spotless," Sophia cried. "If you clean anymore, you're going to take the finish off the wood."

"I will be tired after the week of work," she said. "I think I will not want to go anywhere."

"We'll do everything," Sophia said. "We'll fix the food and pack up the car. You don't have to do anything but come with us. It will be a good way to relax."

Mrs. Rizzo turned away. "We'll see," she said.

The Wakefields were gathered in the living room that evening after dinner. Mr. Wakefield sat reading the paper, and Mrs. Wakefield was working on a crossword puzzle. Jessica and Steven were playing a game of checkers, and Elizabeth was flipping through her social studies book.

Suddenly, Mr. Wakefield began to laugh.

"What's so funny?" Mrs. Wakefield asked.

Mr. Wakefield was laughing so hard he couldn't speak.

"What's the joke, Dad?" Steven asked.

"Listen to this," he said when he finally caught his breath. "It's an open letter to the residents of Sweet Valley." He gave Jessica an odd look, then he began to read:

> To the residents of Sweet Valley, from Quake-Field Wakefield. Dear Sweet Valley. Yesterday I received a petition from the students at Sweet Valley Middle School begging me not to continue an ancient family feud. The petition had many signatures, and the framers of the document seemed genuinely troubled by what they perceived as a rift in my family. I hope that this letter will put their minds at rest. Every member of my family and I are on excellent terms. And though the Wakefields may not be as fortunate, their family differences are not my concern. My name is not really Wakefield. It is Frankenhuysen. It is a fine name, and I am proud of it. But it is difficult to pronounce and even harder to spell. Like many public figures, I chose to use a "stage name." Since "Quake-Field" has been my nickname since Little League, I decided to use "Wakefield" along with it. It rhymes and it's easy to remember. I apologize for any confusion this may have caused and I extend my best wishes to the real Wakefields, whoever they are.

Steven was howling with laughter, and Mrs. Wakefield and Elizabeth were doubled over by the time Mr. Wakefield finished.

Jessica sat in the middle of the floor in stunned silence. Her face was as red as a tomato.

"I think I detect the hand of Jessica Wakefield in this somewhere," Mr. Wakefield said. "Care to explain?"

"I'm dead," Jessica shrieked. "I'm going to have to change my name and move to another town!"

"If you're going to change your name, why don't you change it to Frankenhuysen?" Steven managed to choke out between guffaws.

"I think I'm beginning to understand your sudden interest in genealogy, Jessica," Mrs. Wakefield said, laughing. "You told everyone we were related to Quake-Field Wakefield, didn't you? And you made up some story about a family feud to explain why you couldn't get box seats at the game. Am I close?"

Jessica hung her head in shame. "Please don't give me a lecture about lying. I'll never tell another lie again as long as I live, I promise!"

"Uh-oh," Steven put in. "That sounds like another lie already. I'll bet you're already thinking up some story to get you out of this at school."

"I am not!" Jessica shouted. But the flush on her face told everyone that Steven was right. She shook her head. "I'll never live this down," she wailed. "Never. I'll be the laughingstock of the whole school."

"Actually," Mrs. Wakefield said mildly, "you might have been right all along."

Everyone turned to stare at her.

"What are you talking about?" Jessica said.

Everyone was silent as Mrs. Wakefield walked to the bookshelf and took down a thick volume. "I think my great-grandmother's maiden name was Frankenhuysen. I'm serious. Maybe we really are related."

Mrs. Wakefield flipped quickly through the pages of her own family's genealogy. "Yes. Here it is. Frankenhuysen. My father's father's mother's maiden name. And they settled here in California. I'll bet there is a connection."

"No way," Steven said.

"There's only one way to find out," Mr. Wakefield said, going to the phone. He looked in the telephone book for the number. Then he called the clubhouse and asked to speak to Quake-Field Wakefield.

They all held their breath as they waited to see if he would get through.

"My name is Ned Wakefield," they heard him explain, "and I think I can clear up the mystery of the Wakefield family feud."

After a few minutes, they heard him introducing himself again. Then he launched into the story. From time to time, they heard a booming laugh coming from the receiver.

"He thinks it's funny," Jessica said breathlessly. "That's a good sign—I hope."

Soon, Mr. Wakefield was laughing, too. When he got to the part about Mrs. Wakefield's great-grandmother, he motioned for his wife to take the phone.

Mrs. Wakefield introduced herself and then listened. "That's right," they heard her say. "Clara Frankenhuysen. In California." She laughed. "Well, it's nice to meet you, too, Cousin Quake-Field." She listened for a few more minutes, and then she motioned to Jessica. "He wants to talk to you."

Jessica swallowed hard. "I hope I'm not going to get yelled at by a famous baseball player," she said.

Mrs. Wakefield handed Jessica the phone. "Hello?" she said shyly.

Jessica began to smile. Then she giggled. Then she laughed.

"Unbelievable," Steven said to Elizabeth. "Only Jessica could make up an outrageous lie and have it turn out to be true. There's no justice in this world."

"Shhhh," Elizabeth said, turning her attention back to Jessica. But she couldn't help laughing. Her twin had more nerve than any six people put together.

"Cousin Quake-Field," Elizabeth heard her ask, "how do you feel about recycling?"

Jessica and Quake-Field spoke for a few more minutes and then Jessica hung up. "It's in the bag," she told her family with a grin. "He's going to come to school on Saturday to pose and sign autographs. He said he also wants to have his picture taken with me and Elizabeth for the paper."

Everybody cheered but Steven.

"It's not fair!" he yelled. "You guys get away with everything. Somebody up there likes you two—and they have *terrible taste*."

The twins laughed. "Oh, shut up," they said together.

Fourteen

◇

Mrs. Rizzo sat on a blanket in the park. "I still think it is silly for you to bring me here today," she complained. "I am so tired and not good company."

"You'll get your energy back if we take a walk," said Tony eagerly.

"No," said Mrs. Rizzo. "You go with your sister. I will sit here."

"Please come with us, Mama. PLEASE!" Sophia grabbed her mother's hand and pulled her to her feet.

"But I don't want to walk," grumbled Mrs. Rizzo.

"Just a short walk," Tony pleaded. "Only as far as the duck pond."

Sophia and Tony led their reluctant mother through the woods. The duck pond was in the meadow just beyond the trees. Sophia's eyes anxiously searched the sky. She hadn't spoken to Sarah that day, so she didn't know exactly what to expect. She saw Tony watching the sky, too.

"That's enough," Mrs. Rizzo said. "Let's go back."

Sophia and Tony shared a nervous glance.

Suddenly Sophia heard her mother gasp. She followed the direction of her mother's eyes and saw what she had been searching for. It was a kite. A bright pink kite with a fierce dragon on it.

Mrs. Rizzo stood there frozen for a moment. Then she began to run through the trees toward the kite.

Sophia and Tony ran behind her. Suddenly, they saw the meadow through a break in the trees. Mrs. Rizzo ran out of the dark woods toward Mr. Thomas, who stood beside Sarah on the sunny expanse of green grass.

Mr. Thomas quickly handed the end of the string to Sarah. Then he caught Mrs. Rizzo up in his arms and twirled her around.

Sophia, Sarah, and Tony laughed and applauded.

"It worked," Sophia said through her tears. "You did it."

Sarah smiled at Sophia. "*We* did it," she said.

Sophia extended her hand toward Sarah. "Shake?"

Sarah shook her head. "Hug," she said.

The two girls hugged and then laughed as they heard Tony groan.

"Cut it out, everybody. Please cut it out."

"He's such a tough guy," Sophia teased.

Mr. Thomas and Mrs. Rizzo finally broke apart. "I'd say this calls for a celebration. Who wants ice cream?" Mr. Thomas asked.

Sarah spoke up at once. "I do."

"I'd rather have pizza," Sophia said.

The two girls exchanged a glare.

"Ice cream," insisted Sarah.

"OK, ice cream," Sophia agreed.

Sarah put her hands on her hips. "No. Let's do what you want. We'll go for pizza."

"If you want ice cream," Sophia said irritably, "then let's get ice cream."

Before they could exchange another word, they saw Tony and their parents moving toward them.

"Oh, no," they both said when they looked behind them and saw the duck pond.

"This time we'll do it ourselves," Sophia said. She grabbed Sarah's hand.

"ONE . . . TWO . . . THREE . . ." they chanted together. And on the count of three, they raced toward the duck pond.

"HOOORAYYY!" they shouted. Then, still holding hands, they jumped in—together.

It looked like a carnival at Sweet Valley Middle School on Saturday afternoon. Students, parents, and teachers had all turned out to welcome Quake-Field Wakefield.

He arrived right on time, wearing his uniform. Everybody cheered when he stepped out of the car. He immediately spotted Jessica and Elizabeth in the crowd. "Well, how are my twin cousins?" he said with a big smile.

He was so large that he made even Jessica feel shy. But he was so friendly and happy to meet everyone that it wasn't long before they were treating him like an old friend.

Jessica introduced Quake-Field to Ken and Lloyd.

"I certainly want to thank you two for bringing our family together," Quake-Field said, grinning.

The boys grinned back. "Are you ready to pose?" Ken asked.

"You bet," Quake-Field replied.

The boys had pinned a huge piece of paper to an outside wall of the gym. They handed Quake-Field a soda can and posed him in front of a recycling bin.

Then they began to draw. Amazingly enough, they actually got a good likeness.

To top off the day, the photographer from the newspaper took a picture of Jessica, Elizabeth, Ken, Lloyd, and Quake-Field standing in front of the mural for the Sunday supplement.

"What a wonderful day," Jessica said, hugging herself. She, Elizabeth, Lila Fowler, and Melissa McCormick were sitting on the field, watching the last of the crowd drift away. "I can't wait to see my picture in the Sunday paper."

Elizabeth giggled. "Me, either. Let's just hope they don't switch our names in the caption."

Jessica stood up and brushed the grass off of her skirt. "Let's go to Casey's and celebrate," she said.

"Good idea," Elizabeth said. "I'm starved."

Melissa stood up. "Me, too."

"Are you coming, Lila?" Jessica asked.

"I don't think so," Lila answered. "I . . . uh . . . don't have any cash on me."

Jessica's eyes widened in surprise. Lila Fowler had more spending money than all of the Unicorns put together. "*What* did you say?"

Lila frowned. "I said I don't have any money with me. My dad is out of town. Usually, he leaves my allowance in the front hall. But this time he didn't." Lila frowned again and studied her fingernails. "I'm sure he just forgot," she said.

"Of course he forgot," Jessica said impatiently. "He'll give it to you as soon as he gets back. So in the meantime, you can borrow some money from me."

Lila looked hesitant. "OK," she said finally. "But I'll just borrow enough for a soda."

Jessica looked at her strangely. Lila usually ordered the most expensive thing on the menu.

"I don't know when he's coming back," Lila explained with a casual shrug. But her face wore a troubled look.

What's wrong with Lila? Find out in Sweet Valley Twins No. 63, POOR LILA!